When a
WOMAN RISES

When a
WOMAN RISES

CHRISTINE EBER

CINCO PUNTOS PRESS ✿ EL PASO, TEXAS

FIRST EDITION
10 9 8 7 6 5 4 3 2 1

Library of Congress Cataloging-in-Publication Data

Names: Eber, Christine Engla, author.
Title: When a woman rises / by Christine Engla Eber.
Description: First edition. | El Paso, Texas : Cinco Puntos Press, [2018]
Identifiers: LCCN 2018008855| ISBN 9781941026779 (hardback : alk. paper) |
  ISBN 9781941026847 (paperback : alk. paper)
Subjects: LCSH: Tzotzil women—Mexico—Chenalho—Social conditions—Fiction. Chenalho (Mexico)—Social conditions—Fiction. | LCGFT: Novels.
Classification: LCC PS3605.B463 W47 2018 | DDC 813/.6--dc23
LC record available at https://lccn.loc.gov/2018008855

Lucia's prayer beginning on page 143 borrows from portions of a prayer against envy spoken by Manuel Cura, a well-respected j'ilol in Chenalhó. The prayer was recorded by Christine Eber over several hours on the night of August 25, 1987.

Book and cover design by Paco Casas and Edgar Amaya of
Blue Panda Design Studio

May we all rise in celebration!

WHEN A WOMAN RISES, NO MAN IS LEFT BEHIND

WHY WOULD AN anthropologist decide to write a novel? Because Christine Eber is always pushing herself to help the rest of us understand the modern Tsotsil Maya people, people she has been learning from for over thirty years. What she describes in *When A Woman Rises* is not a static world of traditional people untouched by outside forces, but a community of men and women actively struggling to make their way in the world we all share, to live decent lives not only according to their interpretation of the lessons passed down to them but in response to the new challenges they must face each day. How can they promote peace and justice where so much inequality and violence exist? How can they survive economically when they don't have access to necessary land or education? How can they do things differently without provoking the envy or hatred of neighbors? How can a woman rise in a way that helps men rise with her?

Christine Eber has practiced 'love' in the Mayan sense of the word, which means— according to the book's narrator Magdalena—listening deeply, not giving up on each other, helping each other, respecting each other, and feeling each other's pain. This Mayan word for love is 'our heart hurts,' *k'ux ko'onton*, a deep love that leads to two-way understanding.

—DIANE RUS
author of *Mujeres de tierra fría: conversaciones con las coletas*

TO GABRIEL & KRISHNA

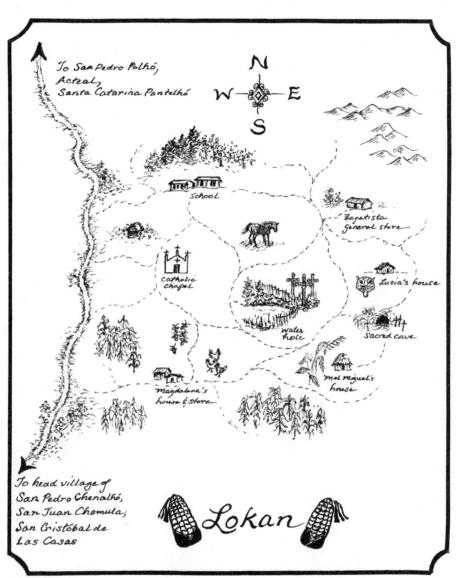

To San Pedro Polhó,
Acteal,
Santa Catarina Pantelhó

N
W · E
S

school

Zapatista
General store

Lucia's house

Catholic
chapel

water
hole

Sacred cave

Mol Miguel's
house

Magdalena's
house & store

To head village of
San Pedro Chenalhó,
San Juan Chamula,
San Cristóbal de
Las Casas

Lokan

Map by Christine Eber

WE BEGIN

IT'S BEEN ELEVEN YEARS since Lucia disappeared. Every day I've waited, hoping to hear her voice from the half open doorway calling, "Are you there? I've come." But she never came, and the days passed, and it was as if she no longer existed.

I tried to convince her not to go, to stay here. "You've got to stay on the land, you've got to keep struggling with us," I told her. But Lucia couldn't take it anymore, and she left one rainy November day.

This year on Feast of the Souls—or Day of the Dead, as the mestizos call it—I decided to do something different, to break with tradition a little. So, when we were placing the wooden chairs in front of our home altar to welcome back the souls of our dead relatives, I put a chair there for Lucia. We'd welcome her soul from wherever it was to come back to us this day, to share our tamales and beef soup, the bounty of our labors here in this place of her ancestors.

And so we did, and none of my family scolded me. My husband Victorio just looked deeply into the fire when I told him who the chair was for.

That day I couldn't stop thinking about Lucia. Each time I put more food on the table in front of her chair, I remembered that she would always bring a gift of food to us: three or four eggs wrapped in corn husks or a kettle of cooked squash—my favorite treat in harvest season. Then she would sit down by the fire in our kitchen and pull a blouse out of her string bag to embroider while we talked.

I remember how she looked sitting on that very chair talking to me.

She was too thin to be really pretty, but the smile in her eyes made her face comfortable and easy to look at. When I said something that she found funny, she would bend over so her head was on top of her knees, and her whole body would shake with laughter. Her loosely braided hair would fall around her shoulders and down her shawl.

My daughter Verónica was just six years old when we last saw Lucia, the same age I was when Lucia and I first met. My daughter loved it when Lucia came to visit us. While we talked and laughed, she would listen to us and pretend to weave with my discarded threads.

Now Verónica is a woman, all grown up. On this Day of the Dead, she started to talk to me about Lucia. She wanted to know all about her life, but I was too busy serving food to visitors to answer her questions.

If only I could have stayed busy forever! But I had no good excuse not to talk about Lucia when Verónica came to ask again. She actually had a very good reason.

A few weeks before Day of the Dead, she had gotten her first part-time job collecting the stories of women in our township. Telling Our Stories, the organization that hired her, said they would make a book of the best stories that were gathered.

They gave her a tape recorder and taught her how to record the women's voices. Little by little my daughter learned to use the machine. First she recorded her own voice, then she asked me to talk into the machine so she could practice asking questions.

I was embarrassed to hear my voice. I sounded like someone else! But I told myself that if I had to suffer a little, it was worth it because my daughter was earning a bit of money.

I didn't see it coming: one day we stopped practicing. She asked me if she could record me for the book, if I would tell my story. She used our tradition of giving a bottle of soda or pox, our homemade rum, to ask for a favor. Since we don't drink, she brought me an orange-flavored Fanta from the little store that Victorio built next to our house. I accepted the soda so as not to disrespect the gift, but I told her, "Daughter, I can't do this. I'm too busy for experiments. And my life isn't that interesting."

"But, Mother," she protested, "that's not true. And you can talk while you're weaving or making tortillas, or when we're tending our store together. I promise not to interrupt your work that much."

I didn't want to disappoint my daughter, so finally I agreed. But I told her that I wouldn't tell my own story. No. I would tell the story of my comadre, Lucia. After all, she wanted to know more about Lucia. And Lucia's life was worth telling.

One afternoon not long after Feast of the Souls when we were waiting in our store for customers, Verónica put the tape recorder on a little table and pulled up two plastic chairs. After we sat down, she took a pen and wrote very carefully in her notebook, "Lucia Pérez López' story, as told by Magdalena to her daughter, Verónica, on November 12th, 2007."

Once I began to talk, Lucia's story flowed out of me like water from a swollen stream. I was surprised that so much of Lucia was stored up inside me, wanting to come out! I started with my first memories of her, when we were little girls playing after church on Sundays. Verónica touched the red button on her tape recorder. I wrapped my shawl tightly around my chest and began.

FRIENDS

WHEN WE WERE LITTLE it wasn't common to spend time with friends outside of church or school. Did you ever wonder why our language doesn't have a word for "friends"? Perhaps the Maya ancestors didn't think we needed one, because our lives are filled with relatives. Mothers, fathers, brothers, sisters, cousins, aunts, uncles, grandparents, godmothers, godfathers. You know how it is. Relatives constantly help one another. They bring tortillas when there's sickness, help at births, take care of nieces and nephews. We visit when there's a reason. Or sometimes, when we miss someone, we make up a reason.

Lucia and I lived on opposite sides of Lokan, but we saw a lot of each other even so. Before we started going to school, we would see each other on Sundays at the old chapel in Lokan. Back then it stood at the top of a little hill in a grove of oak trees. From the outside it looked just like one of our houses, but inside it was a sacred space.

It had an altar that held a statue of the Virgin Mary, candles, and an incense burner. Whenever I entered, there was always a little scent of copal in the air because healers often came there to light incense and pray. In front of the altar were rows of benches.

Just like today, the women sat on one side and the men on the other.

The chapel had a thatch roof. During mass Lucia and I watched for rats to come out from their hiding places in the roof instead of listening to the preacher. We had to stifle our giggles when we saw one.

While we were acting like little girls, my parents and Lucia's mother were listening with their whole hearts to the word of God. They were Believers. Now, when people ask us what our religion is, we say we're Catholic, or Pueblo Creyente, or that we're in the Word of God, but during that time we were just Believers.

I wonder what made my parents want to believe. Maybe it was because they learned that God didn't like it that the rich commanded the poor. It must have made them very excited to think that they could change that. But I wonder why they opened their hearts to listen to the word of God in the beginning.

After mass Lucia and I would play outside with the other children while our parents talked. We made a game of tying the ends of our shawls together and then taking an end and running around the church yard, trying to make the other one fall.

Back then, all of us girls wore traditional shawls, skirts, and blouses, but they were very simple compared to the ones we wear today. We didn't have many colored threads to choose from then or much money or time to spend on decorating our clothes. So our clothes only had a few designs.

We were lucky if we had two skirts and two blouses: one for church and school and one to change into after school. I remember I felt bad for Lucia because she only had one skirt and a blouse. They were made of the sacks that they used to put flour in. Her blouse had only two or three designs because her mother didn't know how to weave, just embroider.

Lucia was different from the other girls. She didn't seem ashamed of her blouse made from a flour sack or her mended skirt—or anything for that matter. When we were learning castellano in school, she would be the first to raise her hand and blurt out the word to the teacher. She didn't pronounce it correctly, but she was close enough for the teacher to understand.

While the other girls hid behind their shawls when the teacher asked questions, I started to copy Lucia and raise my hand too. We passed messages between us written on the palms of our hands. We wrote them in bats'i k'op even though we didn't know how to write correctly in our language. We just wrote how the words sounded, the way the teacher taught us to do in castellano. Lucia figured it out, and then I watched how she did it.

We also wrote Spanish words in our hands, especially ones that ended in "ita." We liked how they looked and sounded when we whispered them. Like when a mestiza mother says, "mi hijita" to show she is fond of her daughter. But we liked the endings of words in bats'i k'op the best, like when something is plural. We would put "etike" on the end of all the words we could think of, like *antsetike* for more than one woman or *vinikitike* for more than one man.

We had fun talking in plural all the time. It was like making the trees burst into bloom all around us.

Maestro Moreno didn't know how to teach well. Even when he made sense, I didn't hear him because I couldn't stop thinking about his crooked nose. He must have broken it, and when it healed, it didn't line up straight. I kept wanting to straighten Maestro Moreno's nose!

The worst days were when Maestro Moreno came to school drunk. Then his nose would be swollen and red, as well as crooked. His eyes would be yellow, but most of the time we couldn't see them because he kept them half-closed as he talked. Most days he spoke in a mixture of castellano and tsotsil, but when he was drunk he only spoke in castellano, and we could barely understand him.

We children were afraid of drunks because you never know what they'll do. Some would just talk a lot, sing songs, or cry. But others might get really angry and hit you if you got in their way. Maestro Moreno had done all of those things at one time or another. So we would sit very still on our benches and watch him closely.

One day he was really drunk. He stood up to teach, but made no sense. He mumbled and tipped back and forth on his feet. I was scared he would fall! Luckily, before he did, he pulled a chair toward him, managed to sit down in it, and passed out. Just like that!

One minute he was talking and the next he was slumped over like a dead man. We looked at each other not sure what to do. We sat still as stones. It was so quiet in the room you could hear the sound of leaves outside the window rustling in the breeze.

Finally, my cousin Fernando stood up on the boys' side of the room and asked, "Is he dead?"

Lucia and I sat in the first row of the girls' side. Before I knew it, Lucia was standing next to the teacher with her little fingers fanned out in front of his mouth to see if there was any air coming out. "He's breathing!" she announced. But she wasn't content just to make that discovery.

Next thing I knew she was tapping Maestro Moreno on his shoulder. She tapped and tapped, but nothing happened. He didn't wake up. Finally, she turned around and faced us as if she were a teacher making an important announcement.

"Maestro Moreno is passed out, and he probably won't wake up for a long time." We gathered up our pencils and notebooks and ran out of the classroom, scattering like feathery seeds that the wind carries away.

For the rest of the day, Lucia and I played hide and seek among the banana trees until it was time to go home.

Home. We spent so much time there when we were little. My mother often kept me home from school so I could take care of my younger sister while she wove or went up the hill to wash clothes. I knew she needed to weave to make money to buy the food we couldn't grow ourselves, but I was angry because I wanted to be in school with Lucia and the other children.

I didn't stay angry with my mother very long. I thought she was the most beautiful person in the world. Her black hair had a little red in it, and she had freckles on her face and arms, just like you, Verónica.

Now her hair is grey, and she has those white patches on her skin. But people take note of her and what she says, at least people in our community.

I don't think Lucia had missed a day of school during our first years. Her mother wanted her to go to school because Lucia was intelligent, and she thought she could go far in school and get a job like the mestizos. Lucia's mother only had a little land. To get food, Lucia and her mother worked in other people's fields and were paid with corn, beans, and squash at harvest time. They raised chickens too and sometimes bartered eggs for salt, sugar, blankets, and other things they needed.

Back then, we didn't know a lot about raising chickens, and they often died of cholera. So we couldn't always count on eating eggs or making money from selling them. Sometimes I'd wake up in the morning, and it would be so quiet. No roosters would be crowing like we were accustomed to in the morning.

Once when we had the most chickens we'd ever had, one by one they all got cholera and died. I remember the morning the last chick died. Mother yelled out in desperation, "Why couldn't cholera have come when I only had a few chickens, instead of now when I have the most chickens I've ever had?" But after the chickens died there was more corn for us.

Everyone was poor back then, but Lucia and her mother were extra poor. Nobody had many possessions, but Lucia's mother's kitchen only had the most basic utensils. A hand grinder for corn stood on top of a wood stand in one corner. The only other pieces of furniture were two small tables for eating, a few wood blocks for sitting, and one little wooden chair for her grandfather who lived with them.

The walls didn't have many things stacked against them. Only a few net bags hung from the rafters.

Lucia's mother had one small clay griddle, while my mother had a huge griddle to make all the tortillas for our family of five. We had a lot of clay pots of different sizes and several enamel pots and ladles all stacked against the wall or on a big table my father built for us. Lucia's mother only owned a few clay pots and her ladles were made of wood.

In her house everything came from the earth: the clay bowls, the gourds for drinking, net bags made from agave fiber, the little chairs and tables of pine. The walls of Lucia's house were also made of earth, like ours. But the walls in Lucia's kitchen were full of cracks that looked like giant spider webs. Once a big hole opened up in the wall of the kitchen, and, before they could repair it, a dog entered in the night and ate the pieces of beef that Lucia received from the mother of a boy she had prayed for.

But I'm getting ahead of myself.

When I was a girl I loved to be in Lucia's kitchen with just her and her mother and her grandfather, Hilario. He was a very respected healer. Sometimes he sat by the fire with us and made bags of agave fiber that he sold to make a little money.

It was so quiet in Lucia's kitchen. No baby sister crying to be fed or picked up. No big brother—your uncle Ricardo—making me bring him his matz when he could easily take a hunk of ground corn off the grinding table and mix it in water himself. I didn't know if he was treating me like a servant because I was little, or because I was a girl, but since it seemed like everyone expected me to do these things for him, I didn't complain.

I only went to Lucia's house when my mother had some food for me to take to Lucia's mother, Carmela. My mother looked out for Carmela because she was my brother's godmother, and her life was hard without a husband or sons. Lucia's father disappeared when she was about three years old. He went away with a group of men to work on a tomato farm in Sinaloa in the North of Mexico. Her mother and the other wives and families waited for the men to return in six months when they said they would, but the months stretched on to eight, then ten, and finally a year had passed. Some of the relatives went to the authorities in the town center to see if they knew where to find the men. The judge knew the enganchador, the man who contracted for the owner of the ranch where the men went. So the families had a meeting to talk about what to do.

"We've got to go see if they're still there, if they're prisoners of the landowner, or what's happening to them," the wives said. Then they took up a collection of money among the families and gave it to sons of three of the men so they could go to the ranch and look for their fathers. The boys took a bus that went for many, many hours. They suffered on the trip because they were cold and hungry and worried about what they would find when they got there.

When they arrived at the ranch it was already dark, and they began asking whoever they could find where the enganchador lived. It was late when they finally knocked on his door. No one answered. One of the boys went to the window and saw the engachador sitting at the table eating supper. The boys called to him through the window, "Please, sir, we've come a long way to look for our fathers. They came here to work about a year ago, and we never heard from them again. They never came back to us when they said they would, and we're worried that something has happened to them."

The enganchador put his napkin down, got up from the table, and opened the door. He stood in the doorway towering over the boys who were holding their hats trying to show respect to him. The enganchador just looked puzzled when the boys handed him a piece of paper with the men's names. Then he smiled and said, "No, sons, your fathers aren't here.

I never contracted to bring them here. You must have the wrong ranch. There are a lot of ranches in Sinaloa where men from Chiapas come to work. Or maybe they decided to go work in the United States. You'll have to try one of the other ones. Now I have to get back to my supper."

The boys didn't believe the enganchador, but what could they do after he shut the door in their faces? All they could think to do was go to the nearest town and ask the authorities if they could help them find their fathers. So they found a place to sleep in the fields. Early the next morning they began walking to the town. When they got to the town hall, the authorities didn't want to help them. They told them that the enganchador was telling them the truth, that their fathers had probably gone to the U.S.

"Be patient boys," they said. "Your fathers are probably working on a farm somewhere in the United States, and when they have some money they'll send word to you where they are and when they'll be home. Just wait. You'll see. Now go back home. Your mothers must be worried about you."

How desperate those boys must have felt to hear the mestizos talk about their fathers like stray donkeys that would make their way home in their own time.

To this day we don't know what happened to Lucia's father and the other men. We think they're dead because they wouldn't have just gone to El Norte without letting us know they're there and how they are. They had debts to pay and families to take care of. They only went to make some money and then come back home. Who knows how they died or if they are prisoners somewhere? Only God knows. But we don't stop praying for them. At mass each Sunday, the prayer leaders still ask God to take care of our compañeros who left in search of work and if they are alive to bring them back to us.

When we pray our separate prayers, I ask God to bring Lucia back.

A DREAM LIKE NO OTHER

A NEIGHBOR CAME into our store. Verónica quickly covered the tape recorder with a tortilla cloth. I had asked her not to talk about our project so she always covered the tape recorder when people came into the store.

It's been a while since we've covered our TV with a cloth so not to draw attention to it when visitors come. But it seems that whenever we buy something that costs a lot of money, or we start to do something different, we try to disguise it so our neighbors won't think that we're proud of our possessions or what we're doing.

It's that old envy problem, complicating our lives...

I helped our neighbor pick out some thread for a blouse she was weaving while Verónica tidied up a shelf of canned sardines.

After our neighbor left, Verónica said, "Mother, how do people go on without knowing where their loved ones are? Lucia didn't remember what it was like to have a father, but I couldn't bear to think about Father disappearing. We've been together all my life. Sometimes when he's gone for two or three days to attend a meeting of the Believers or the Zapatistas, I miss him. When he comes home, he tells us everything that happened.

"When I was a little girl I would sit for hours with my face in my hands and my elbows on my knees taking in every word he said. His voice is one I carry with me in my head along with yours and Abolino's and Sebastian's. But if he were gone a long time, like Lucia and her father, maybe I wouldn't hear his voice anymore.

"Mother, do you still hear Lucia's voice?"

I thought for a moment. "Yes, I still hear Lucia's voice when I talk about her. It's a part of her that lives on and helps me tell her story. It's as if she's here with me when I remember the things she said. But now I need to tell you about something important that happened to Lucia when she was about ten years old."

Verónica took the tortilla cloth off the tape recorder. I cleared my throat and began to talk about Lucia's grandfather who knew how to heal people.

 When he was alive, Lucia's grandfather healed hundreds of people. If he couldn't help them, he would tell them to go to the clinic in the lum, the center of our township, where all the government offices and workers were.

Hilario was committed to his calling. People would come to his door in the middle of the night asking him with great humility, but much urgency, to come pray for their sick family member. He would ask what was wrong with the person. If it was something he could cure, he would go right away to the person's house, walking with a torch, sometimes for miles on steep mountain trails.

Lucia wanted to go with her grandfather when he went to pray for people, and he often let her. Many times Hilario came to our house to pray for someone in our family who was sick. During the healing—which would last for many hours—I would sit next to Lucia in the corner of our kitchen while one of my parents or my siblings was lying on a straw mat by the fire.

At first, Hilario would tell Lucia to lay out the candles, pine boughs, incense, and bottles of pox at the head of the sick person. After the candles were lit, and Hilario had begun to pray, Lucia would go back to her place in the corner and pray softly under her shawl along with her grandfather.

Lucia had a mind like your tape recorder. It was as if she hit a button in her heart—when her grandfather started to pray, she would press it and the words got engraved in her heart. Hilario and the other elders told us that thoughts and feelings start in the heart, then go to the mind, and finally come out the mouth. That's how Lucia learned everything important in our traditions, by recording them in her heart where they spread roots and then came out in words, which had power.

Sometimes when Lucia and I walked home from school, we would veer off into the forest where the pitch pine trees grow. There Lucia would practice praying to cure me even though I wasn't sick.

I would lie down among the trees and pretend I was sick while Lucia collected pine boughs and laid them out on the ground near my head. My pine needle bed was soft. We didn't have any candles, incense, or pox, so Lucia substituted sticks for candles and pine cones for incense.

Before she began to pray, I would look up at her face, which had smoothed out like a piece of cloth waiting for someone to embroider on it. When Lucia bowed her head and her hair fell over her face, I couldn't see her anymore. So I closed my eyes and waited for her to start praying. Her voice was low and slow when she began, but it didn't take long before her words got faster and hotter.

> "This is why I come,
> kneeling with my face to the ground,
> beneath your feet, my Lord,
> and under your hands, my Lord,
> under your shadow, my Lord…
> Holy Mother María,
> Flowery Jesus Christ, my Lord
>
> Look at me, my Lord,
> at your daughter.
> Send me your healing strength.
> Lower it to me.
> Come heal your daughter Magdalena for me.'"

Sometimes I would doze off while Lucia was praying.

One morning Lucia came to school at the last minute just when we were lining up to sing the national anthem. She slipped in the line behind me. I could hear her teeth chattering. I turned to look at her and saw that her hair wasn't combed, and she didn't have her shawl. The pleats in the front of her skirt were falling out of her belt. Her face reminded me of the face of a little kit fox I had surprised on the trail the day before. She had a wild look, as if she had seen things I couldn't imagine, as if she could look further or deeper than I could. I felt as if I had lost my friend: here was another girl pretending to be Lucia, wearing her clothes and talking like her.

When it was time for recess, Lucia took me by the hand and led me to the níspero tree behind the school. We sat down under the tree and she told me what had happened. Little by little, as Lucia told me her story, I felt that I was getting my friend back. But she had changed in ways I couldn't completely understand.

Lucia said to me, "I had a dream last night. It was the third time I've had the same dream. The first and second times I didn't tell anybody, not even you, because I was scared and I didn't want to know what my dream meant. But last night the dream came again, and I had to tell my grandfather about it because the Moon Virgin ordered me to. You're the second person I'm telling my dream to. Not even my mother knows."

Then Lucia told me the dream that changed her life.

"In my dream I was asleep, but I had to go to the bathroom really bad. So I went outside and the whole patio was filled with light from the Moon. Our house looked like a beautiful cathedral. The Holy Mother Moon came down to me and almost touched the ground. She had a dark brown face, just like ours, and she wore a blue shawl sprinkled with white stars. She held her hands out to me. They were dark brown too. But I was scared and jumped back.

"Then Mother Moon talked to me. 'Daughter, listen to me,' she said. 'Your heart is thinking a lot. What is it you'd like to know?'

"I want to learn to pray," I said.

"'Good. If it's true that you want to learn to pray, then you have to pay attention. First you're going to take a little gourd of water, a ball of ground corn, your little net bag, your candles, your incense, your pine branches, your pox.'

"Alright. I'll take them," I said, because I was too afraid not to obey her.

"'That's good,' she said. 'You're going to take them so that you can heal with them. But you're not ready yet. You need to learn the prayers.'

"That's alright. I'll learn them." Since I already knew a few prayers

I thought I could learn the rest.

"'Good,' she said. 'Now go ask your grandfather to help you.'

"That's what the Moon Virgin said to me. When I woke up this morning, I could still hear her words, but my dream was covering me like an extra blanket that was so heavy I couldn't breathe. I was afraid because I remembered my grandfather's story of when Saint Peter came to him. My grandfather didn't want to believe the dream the first time the apostle came, but then St. Peter came a second time and said the same thing, except with more force. Still, my grandfather didn't accept the dream. When St. Peter came the third time, he knew he had to accept it in his heart.

"It was still night. My mother and grandfather were snoring. I just lay in bed until my mother woke up and went to the kitchen. I had to tell my grandfather about my dream, so I went to his bed and patted him on the shoulder. He woke up and rubbed his eyes and then he asked me, 'Why are you up so early, granddaughter?' I told him about what the Moon Virgin told me in my dreams. My grandfather said, 'So it is, so it is,' many times while I was talking. When I finished, he said, 'Grandaughter, if the dream had only come once or twice, you could ignore it, but it came three times, and that means that you must do what the Moon Virgin tells you to do. You must accept your cargo. You must learn to heal. You must learn to be an j'ilol, one who sees what illness has entered a person.'"

Then Lucia said that she told her grandfather she was ready to accept her cargo. He said that they would have to seal the agreement with the Virgin right away. They got dressed quickly. Hilario told Lucia's mother that Lucia had asked to go to the church to pray before school. Although she had never done this before, her mother didn't say anything, except not to forget her shawl. But Lucia was already running to catch up with her grandfather on the trail and didn't want to go back.

Then Lucia went on to tell me what happened in the church.

"At the church we knelt in front of the statue of the Virgin Mary while my grandfather prayed to the Moon Virgin, to St. Peter, to Earth, and to the Father-Mother-Ancestor-Protectors to give me strength in my legs to walk long distances and in my whole body to bear the cold, rain, and hunger. He asked the Moon to keep my heart strong and to give it courage not to give in to the one who comes behind, who wants to use our power for evil and tricks people into serving him. He asked her to forgive me for not covering my head, that I was still young and needed to learn how to serve her with respect.

"I was shivering in the church beside my grandfather like I'm shivering now. But I'm not cold because I don't have my shawl, I'm trembling because I'm afraid. I'm just a little girl, but the Moon Virgin wants me to heal! What will my life be like now? Can I still go to school? I want to heal and also keep learning."

Lucia had had a cargo dream, the special dream that calls us to serve our people as healers, midwives, or leaders of fiestas. People don't have them that often today, but when I was growing up many people had cargo dreams. After such dreams they became different from the rest of us. Lucia's dream gave her power to talk directly to God, the Moon Virgin, and all the spiritual beings.

I wanted to make Lucia feel better so I said, "Maybe you can just go along with your grandfather and learn from him like you've been doing, and then after you graduate from primary school, you can heal anytime you're needed because you won't be in school. Ah, but you want to go on in school, don't you?"

Lucia nodded her head. She didn't want to remind me that I wouldn't be able to go to school past sixth grade because my parents didn't want me to live in the city. But if she became a healer, Lucia wouldn't have the freedom to study because she would have to stay in the community. We were just little girls, but we were already thinking about our future. And it seemed that there were big logs blocking our way.

MY COUSIN ROSA

AFTER LUCIA HAD HER DREAM, I would often go to her house with a gift of food, and she wouldn't be there. I would come to the door and ask, "Are you there?" Her mother would tell me to come in, and my heart would sink a little because she was all alone embroidering by the fire. I would just give the food to Lucia's mother, but she wouldn't let me leave without my own gift of food. As is our custom, she would fill two tortillas with beans and give the little package to me to eat on my way home or later when I was hungry. If she didn't have any beans, she would fill the tortillas with cooked greens.

When I saw Lucia again at school, she always told me where she and her grandfather had gone and what happened during the healing. I listened closely because I envied Lucia. I was always hungry for meat. We only had it on Day of the Dead or when there was a healing in our house and my mother had to feed the healer some chicken. I imagined Lucia eating chicken or beef soup at the house of the sick person. My mouth watered thinking of her slurping up the broth with toasted tortillas and tearing the meat off a chicken leg. Sometimes Lucia would bring a piece of beef wrapped in a tortilla to school the next day and share it with me. Even when our lives were becoming so different, she didn't forget me.

In that time, envy was a very dangerous thing. I tried not to envy Lucia, but it took all my strength. When we were little girls, it was rare for people to have meat to eat because they didn't have money to buy bulls. So when someone in our community got money from working somewhere and bought things—like a bull, a burro, or a horse—others envied them for having something they didn't.

Sometimes they would just gossip about the person saying things like, "He must be working for the government. They gave him money to tell them what to do so they could come in and take our land away from us." But at times they went as far as to ask a powerful j'ilol to pray that something really bad would happen to the person, to show them they weren't more important than the rest of us, just because they had money.

I never did anything like that, but I did pray to God to give me a dream like Lucia's so I could be special like her. But if I had had a cargo dream, who could have helped me learn to heal? My grandfather drank a lot and didn't remember what the ancestors told us, or how they used to pray, or maybe he just didn't care about the traditions anymore. I couldn't ask Hilario because he was already teaching Lucia. So I waited for a dream that never came, all the while knowing that even if I got it, I wouldn't know what to do with it.

I contented myself with listening to Lucia's stories about the healings that she went to with her grandfather. Sometimes I happened to be at a sick person's house when Lucia and her grandfather came to pray.

One time I went with my mother to see my cousin Rosa who was very sick. For many weeks she had had a high fever and was sweating a lot. Her mother kept her home from school because Rosa was too tired to get out of bed. Rosa didn't want to eat and just stayed in bed all day. The only thing she wanted to eat was eggs, so my aunt fed her eggs when the chickens were laying. Rosa was as thin as a pile of sticks. My aunt tried to take her to the mestizo doctor at the clinic, but my uncle stopped her when she was waving down a truck in the road. My uncle said that he didn't trust doctors, they just took all your money, and then later you died anyway. Better to bring a traditional healer, he said. He would ask Hilario to come and pray for Rosa. Lucia came too. She and her grandfather arrived just before us.

My aunt was sitting beside Rosa's bed crying into her shawl. My uncle was drinking pox in the corner. Rosa was lying on the bed, just a little bump under the blanket. Lucia and I went close to her face to tell her we had come. She was sweating a lot and smelled like sour fruit. We backed away. We couldn't help ourselves. Later after the prayer was finished, Lucia asked her grandfather why Rosa smelled sour. He said that there is a disease that makes people smell that way and that maybe Rosa had it.

Hilario and my aunt talked a long time while Lucia and I sat and stared at Rosa. I thought about how we three girls were just beginning our lives, and yet one of us looked and smelled like a rotten apple. Is this what it's like to be on the way to dying? I asked myself. I whispered to Lucia, "Do you think she's going to die?"

"I don't know," she said. That made me think that maybe Lucia is afraid when she prays with her grandfather because she comes right up to the edge of the chasm between life and death—maybe she sees death coming, crossing the bridge and there's nothing she can do to stop it.

Ever since I was a little girl, I've been afraid of death. The elders say that everyone has a candle in the sky and that their time will be up when the candle goes out, but I don't believe that. I can't believe that there's a candle for children, especially girls like Rosa who make it all the way to thirteen years old. She was about to graduate from primary school! She had learned the many things a woman needs to do and had her whole life ahead of her. She had a husband to marry and babies to laugh with and teach everything she knew. All of these thoughts were running through my head as we sat and waited.

When he was ready to pray, Hilario told Lucia to put the candles in rows on the ground beside Rosa's bed. It took a while for Lucia to drip bits of wax on the ground to fix each tall white candle in its place and then set pine boughs in front of them. Meanwhile Hilario lit the incense. Prayers need witnesses, and so Lucia, my mother, my uncle, and I took our places on each side of Hilario as he began to pray. He held Rosa's wrist in his hands and felt her pulse. Then Hilario took a cup of pox and made the sign of the cross three times over her chest and three times on each of her sides.

Next my aunt took a white hen that she had been saving for the prayer from under the basket and gave it to Hilario. My aunt helped Rosa into a sitting position and held her while Hilario rubbed the live chicken all around her head and down her shoulders and her sides. Then he pulled the rough blanket off her skirt and rubbed the chicken along the sides of her legs and over her feet. When he was done, he handed the chicken to my aunt. The hen must have known she was going to become our dinner because she was squawking loudly.

Hilario's prayer lasted a long time. Lucia and I got very tired and hungry. When Hilario finally announced, "My prayer is finished," we were relieved because now we could eat. But Hilario looked worried. My aunt and my mother were getting ready to serve the bowls of chicken and broth when Hilario began to talk to my uncle.

"I can see that my prayers aren't entering your daughter's body. I'm sorry that I'm not able to cure her. I would take her to the clinic. If God wants it, the doctors there may be able to treat her illness. I think she may have the disease they call tuberculosis. I've seen people before like your daughter, and that is what the doctors said they had. Some of them got better when they took the medicine."

Rosa's mother was about to set a bowl of soup on the table in front of Hilario. She stood holding the bowl, her eyes red from crying and said, "I wanted to take my daughter to the clinic. I tried. I started to take her there the other day, but my husband stopped me." Rosa's father looked down into his glass of pox and didn't say anything.

The next day my aunt defied my uncle and took Rosa to the clinic in the lum. The doctor examined Rosa, and Hilario was right. It was tuberculosis that was making her so sick. But Rosa's tuberculosis was very advanced. It couldn't be cured in the usual way. Her only hope was to go right away to the hospital in San Cristóbal where they could give her a special treatment. My aunt felt desperate at the doctor's words because she and my uncle owed a lot of people and didn't have any money. My uncle had told my aunt that he would kill her if he found out that Rosa had been taken to a hospital in the city where they would have to pay a lot of money to get her back or maybe they would let her die and demand money anyway. So my aunt just took Rosa home where she died about a week later.

That's how it was back then.

GRADUATION DAY

"MOTHER, WHY DIDN'T ROSA'S MOTHER defy her husband and fight for her daughter's life? If I had been Rosa, you wouldn't have let me die. I'm sure of it."

Verónica had never heard the story of Rosa. I tried to help her understand how it was when we were young.

"Daughter, I want to think that I would have taken you to the hospital even if your father told me not to. But it was different back then. People usually died when they went to the hospital, so we were afraid to take our sick family members there. Also, there weren't any doctors who spoke bats'i k'op and many women didn't know castellano or were embarrassed to speak it. So, when they went to the hospital, they didn't know how to ask for help for their child or for someone to explain to them what was wrong. We felt most comfortable going to our traditional doctors, like Hilario. I know it's hard for you to understand. I thank God that you are living now when we have a little money to take you to a doctor if you have a sickness that we can't heal with plants or prayer."

"I know, Mother. I'm just glad that men aren't so stubborn about being the boss."

"Yes, they've changed. But it took time. Some men still make demands on their wives and daughters that aren't fair. Now, do you want to hear about our graduation day? I remember it as if it was yesterday.

"Yes, Mother. Please begin."

We missed Rosa on graduation day when we lined up on the basketball court in front of our parents and godparents. She should have been standing there with Lucia and me, the three girls in our community who had managed to make it through primary school.

It was hot the day of our graduation. We had to stand a long time on the basketball court without any shade. We girls were dressed in our traditional clothes with ribbons in our hair. Behind us, in a row, stood the six boys who were graduating. The teachers made them wear mestizo clothes: dark pants and a white shirt.

Now that I think about it, those clothes showed what the teachers expected of us, that the boys would find jobs in the world of the mestizos while we girls would stay in the community, marry, and raise children.

Most girls and boys dropped out of school before sixth grade because their parents were too poor to pay their school expenses. Our parents told us that it was enough to learn to read and write a little castellano and to know our numbers so we wouldn't get cheated by the mestizos. Our parents didn't respect or trust the teachers because the teachers didn't know what it was like to get callouses on their hands from working in the fields. They made money just by writing words in notebooks and sitting back while the children copied them or drew pictures.

To our parents these things weren't school. School was learning arithmetic and how to speak a little castellano. When our parents really got angry was when one of the teachers lured away someone's wife. That happened a few times—most of the teachers were men with wives who stayed in the city while their husbands spent the week in the community. They would only go home on weekends. The teachers had little rooms where they slept at the school, but they were always looking for a woman to cook for them and come to their rooms at night.

The teachers taught us how to do special mestizo dances that involved the girls dancing in pairs with boys. Because there were more boys than girls some of the boys had to dance together. Back then the school dances were not at all like the dances at traditional fiestas where everyone just stands where they are, arms at their sides, bouncing back and forth from one foot to the other, as long as the music lasts. I wonder if our people always danced the same? No matter how our traditional dances used to be, we girls were embarrassed to dance both the traditional and mestizo ways.

Our parents and godparents sat around the basketball court watching us dance. The women folded their shawls and put them on top of their heads to shade their eyes from the sun. The men wore their traditional white tunics and hats with colored ribbons and passed around sodas to the people to help them cool off and also because this was a special day. Some of the graduates had mestizo godparents. They held umbrellas over their heads to shade themselves.

My godmother was my Aunt Petra and Lucia's godmother was my mother. When it was time, my aunt, my mother, and the other godparents came onto the court bringing our presents in big wrapped boxes. They stood in a line behind each of us until it was time to escort us off the court to receive our diplomas. My present was a pink sweater. I didn't have a sweater and was very excited to have such a pretty one.

I forgot to tell you that when we were lined up waiting for our godparents, Lucia read the graduation poem. Because she was the smartest in the class, our teacher chose her to write the poem. She had to write it in castellano, and it had to be inspiring but truthful too. She had to memorize it, which wasn't hard for Lucia because she had already memorized many prayers.

The day before, Lucia brought her finished poem to school to show me. I read it. At first it sounded like most graduation poems because it talked about how we were leaving our childhoods behind, and now we were going to be adults. Although we were only thirteen or fourteen years old, it was true that we were now as good as adults because our teachers and parents never encouraged us to go on to middle school— except Lucia's mother, who wanted her to go but didn't have the money to make it happen.

If we had dreams of going on in school, our teachers didn't want to hear them. They only knew that our parents didn't have money to pay for books, food, and to rent a room in San Cristóbal. So how could we do it?

None of our teachers cared enough to help us find money. Or maybe there weren't any scholarships in those days. We surely never heard of any. So, after graduation, the boys began to work full time with their fathers in the fields while we girls helped our mothers with all the work women have to do. And not long after, we married and started having babies.

But Lucia's poem said that young people can do many things besides work in the fields or in the house and marry and have children. We can learn about the world and maybe even write books one day. We can invent machines, design big buildings, and teach children what we know so they can be even smarter and do greater things than we did. I loved Lucia's poem, and when I was done reading it I told her so.

"You wrote what I feel," I said, "that I can do something different from my mother. I want to be a teacher one day, but a much better one than our teachers. We've got to find a way to go to middle school."

I gave Lucia her poem back and she said, "I've been thinking. Maybe we don't need our parents' permission, at least at first. Maybe it's enough to show them how much our hearts want to go to school. They don't know how we yearn to study. Maybe they'll let us work in San Cristóbal to pay our school expenses if they see how determined we are. I've heard that there are mestizas who give girls like us a room and food in exchange for cleaning and cooking. And then, for a few hours a day, they let us go to school. We just need to find two señoras who need maids and live next door so we can see each other every day."

So we hatched our plan that day to run away to San Cristóbal to find work. The next day after the graduation ceremony we toasted on it. While the graduates' mothers were preparing chicken in mole for the whole community, Lucia and I ran off behind the school to a rock where Lucia had hidden a plastic container of pox.

She'd brought it from home from a healing earlier that week. Lucia never drank her portion of pox. Because she was young, it was expected that she would pour her gift of pox into a container to take home to have around in case someone had a cut that needed to be disinfected. This was how she showed her respect for traditions. Lucia had also brought one of her grandfather's shot glasses, and we used it to offer each other little cups of pox.

First Lucia offered me my glass, "Here's your drops from the hands and feet of God," she said. Then I said, "I'm drinking." I didn't like pox because it burned as it went down my throat, but I wanted to drink it, to do something I'd never done before. The container felt lighter and lighter each time we poured another cup until it was light as a feather and no more drops came out. We laughed and rolled on the ground in pleasure.

I don't know how much time passed before our schoolmates found us passed out behind the rock. Our parents came soon after and saw what a pitiful state we were in. One of our schoolmates told us later that when Hilario looked at Lucia sprawled out on the ground, flies licking her lips, he said, "My granddaughter forgot to say in her poem that although young people can do many things, they can also lose their souls along the way."

OUR PATH FORKS

VERÓNICA DIDN'T LET ME forget about my drunken graduation day. She brought it up several times before we sat down to talk about Lucia again. She said things like, "How could you do that, Mother, and then act like you're so perfect? You and Father would kill me if I got drunk, and I'm seventeen! You were only thirteen when you got drunk!"

What Verónica says is true. Her father and I are far from perfect. Although I never drank after my graduation day, Victorio was a drinker before he started listening to the word of God. He used to drink whenever he had money. But it's been thirty years now that he hasn't had a drop of pox, chicha, or beer. God knows we're not without our sins, but we've tried to raise our children to be good people.

It was raining hard the day I took up the topic of Lucia's life after graduation. Verónica and I stood in the doorway of our store watching the patio turn into a muddy lake. Nobody had come to the store since early morning, so we decided to go to the kitchen and warm ourselves by the fire. We covered up with pieces of plastic and raced across the patio to the kitchen. Once inside, I took off my muddy sandals while Verónica rekindled the fire and sat close to the flames to warm herself. I set a basket and some corncobs on the floor between us. While I talked, corn kernels fell from our hands into the basket like little bits of sunshine.

After we graduated, we never left our homes for very long or without a companion. Our days were spent helping our mothers. It was a lot harder back then to keep a family going. We didn't have electric corn grinders like today. All we had were grinding stones or hand grinders to make our tortillas. It would take a few hours every morning to make tortillas and matz—corn gruel—for a large family like ours. We'd begin when it was still dark with only the fire and candles for light. While we'd be patting out our tortillas, we'd listen to the sound of our neighbors making tortillas. If we didn't hear pat-pat, pat-pat coming from a neighbor's house, we'd wonder if she was sick.

The only source of water was the water hole near our house or, when that ran dry, the river. But that was a long way away so we tried not to go there. Every time it rained, we lined up pottery jugs under the roof to gather water. Later, when plastic buckets came to the stores in Chenalhó, we would buy them and line them up too. But we couldn't gather much water that way, not like the rotoplas storage tank that collects water for us now. Thank God for the rotoplas.

I looked at the door and took a long pause. Verónica asked me what I was thinking, so I told her, even though I knew she wouldn't like it.

"I don't know what good it does to talk about the past. I know you want to know about Lucia, but sometimes I feel that what has passed is gone, and it serves no purpose to bring it back."

Verónica looked worried. I didn't want her to think that, just because I didn't want to talk about the past at that moment, I never would talk about it again. She sat still while I looked down at my hands on top of the blouse a neighbor had commissioned me to embroider.

Finally I said, "I'm not going to talk any more about how women worked in the past. You know about it anyway since nothing much has changed except that now we have electricity and cement floors. Sometimes I miss dirt floors. They were easier to clean. We'd just sweep the dirt or pieces of food or corn husks out the door, and the floor would be clean and smooth and warm on our feet. Now we have to wear shoes on the cold cement. If a little child urinates or poops, we can't just dig it up and throw it out the door. We have to fetch a bucket of water and mop it up, sloshing the dirty water around. I know you don't agree, but that's how I feel. Who knows if it was better in the past or today? My head aches thinking about these things.

"But there's something else. I feel badly about things I did before I was married. Telling Lucia's story reminds me of how confused I was back then. I wanted a life different from my mother's, and that made it seem that I didn't respect her. I was afraid that I was losing my soul. It was as if someone was tying up my animal soul companion making me sick.

"Now I feel that that same thing is happening to me. I feel sick from regret about the pain I caused my parents through my actions, through my desires that I didn't control. I can still see my mother and father crying. But I cried too. I cried myself to sleep for a long time after I had to give up my dream of being a teacher. I know you need to know about my story to understand Lucia's, but I have to wait until my sickness passes."

"I'm sorry this is making you sick, Mother. We'll wait and talk again when you're feeling better."

I continued working in the kitchen trying to make my sickness pass while Verónica went back to the store to work on a weaving she'd left on her loom. On the blouse I was embroidering, the black, silver, and gold threads were coming together to make the flowery head of a saint. I liked how the head stood out against the purple and blue striped background. The design made me think of Lucia and me, how we had wanted to stand out too, to have a different life from other women in Lokan. I decided that I should burn a candle and say a prayer to the Virgin Mary. With her help, Our Lord would accept my offering and help me feel free and well again.

Verónica and I stayed apart that afternoon until it was almost dark, and I heard her fasten the latch on the store. By that time my sickness had passed, and I was embroidering the last saint in a row of other saints. Verónica came into the kitchen and quickly pulled a chair near me. "What's that?" she asked. "Oh, nothing, just something I made up." My daughter inspected my work. I was torn between wanting to tell her how I made my new design and getting back to Lucia's story. I decided we could talk about the design tomorrow, so I laid the blouse over the back of my chair, tightened my shawl around me, and said I was ready to talk about Lucia again. I waited while Verónica found the tape recorder and turned it on. I continued with our escape from Lokan when we were just thirteen.

Lucia and I were determined to have different lives from our mothers. So we started to plan our escape, though it was difficult to do that because we knew so little about the city. But we knew one thing for sure—we had to hide it from our parents. This was hard because we had never lied to them, at least not about something important. Being truthful was part of being respectful, and that was very important back then. Except for the day we got drunk, we had been respectful and obedient girls.

So what lies did we tell our parents? Ah, big ones! Totally untrue things. Lucia told her mother that she was going to San Cristóbal with my mother and me and that we would pay her bus fare. I told my mother that Lucia and her mother were going to San Cristóbal to buy medicine for Hilario and that Lucia wanted me to go with them. My mother believed me and gave me bus fare and money to buy rice and thread for our store. I put the money in a change purse and tucked it into the folds of my belt. The money stayed there for a couple days burning a hole in my stomach. I'd never stolen from my mother or anyone.

Once in a dream I stole corn with Lucia. We were yearning to eat fresh corn and our fields didn't have any yet. So, when it was dark, we crept into one of our neighbor's fields and gathered up as many ears of elote as our shawls could hold. A mayol, one of our policemen, saw us scrambling up the hill with corn spilling out of our shawls and yelled for us to stop. Thank God, I woke up before he arrested us and put us in jail! When I realized it was a dream, I felt such relief. That's how much I was afraid of stealing.

When I took my mother's money, I feared that God would punish me severely. Still, I took it.

We decided to go on a Monday. We spent most of Sunday in church with our parents. I prayed to the Moon Virgin to accompany me on the road to San Cristóbal and to take care of me in the city. When we were finally on the bus with our homes disappearing behind us, Lucia told me that late Sunday night, after Hilario and her mother were asleep, she had gone outside to light some candles and pray to the Mother-Father-Ancestor-Protectors to keep our souls from getting lost on the road. Hilario taught Lucia that souls are tied to the place they are born. In order for them to accompany their owners when they travel far away, a special prayer is needed.

I got up about 4 a.m. and tried not to wake my father, my brother, and my little sister. I scooped up my extra skirt and blouse that I used for a pillow and put them in my net bag along with my comb, my graduation sweater, a few pesos I'd saved, and the money my mother gave me. Outside in the dark, I searched for a bucket of water. I found one filled to the brim and splashed the water on my face and feet and smoothed my hair with my wet hands. But it didn't do much good. It had rained heavily in the night, and the mud in our patio just kept sloshing onto my feet.

I hung my bag on a tree branch and went inside the kitchen where Mother gave me a gourd of matz and some toasted tortillas for the road. I drank the matz quickly and said goodbye, nearly forgetting my bag in my rush to meet Lucia. It was still dark when the bus passed on the road below our house about 5 a.m.

We climbed onto the bus, already full with what looked like half of the township! We shared a seat with a woman and her baby. The baby started to cry when we sat down next to her, but Lucia soon turned her tears to smiles by jiggling the tiny gourd rattle hanging from her wrist. Eventually the baby tired of playing and turned to her mother's breast. Her mother pulled a shawl over both their faces and laid her head against the window to get some sleep.

I held onto the back of the seat in front of us to keep from falling into the aisle as the bus swerved from one side of the road to the other to keep from sinking into the holes the rain had left. As the bus lurched ahead, a sick feeling began to take over my whole body. I felt that this was not going to end well, that I was about to feel a level of suffering and sadness that I'd never known.

But Lucia was excited. The whole way to San Cristóbal, she chattered about the things we'd do when we found work and started to go to middle school. She didn't seem worried about what we would do when we arrived in the city, how we would find señoras to work for, where we would sleep that night, and what our parents would do when we didn't come home.

All we knew in San Cristóbal was the cathedral in the center of the city and the market, which is where the bus dropped us off. I'd been in the market many times with my parents, but I always stayed by their side while they talked with the fruit and vegetable vendors. When they climbed the tall sidewalks to enter a store, I'd sit outside on the edge of the sidewalk and tuck my feet under my legs so a truck wouldn't run them over.

My toes curled up when I got off the bus as my bare feet hit the icy cobblestone street. Lucia landed squarely on both feet and grabbed my hand. I thought she would jump for joy when she said, "Look at all the kaxlan ladies!"

Lucia was right, surrounding us were more mestizas than I'd ever seen in one place. They carried baskets and wore black, brown, and grey shawls and were rushing past each other heading for stacks of fruit and vegetables that the people from the country towns were unloading. The oldest ones wore ugly black shoes, but if one of them had given me her shoes I would have gladly worn them!

I think it was fear that made me so cold. I was much more afraid than Lucia. But looking back, maybe we would have been better off had Lucia been more afraid.

I don't know how long we stood there holding hands and watching the people buying and selling everything anyone could need. We were standing next to an atole vendor, and the smell of cinnamon was too much to resist. She was busy trying to keep up with all the people who wanted atole. We got into the line and when our turn came asked for two glasses of rice atole. We held the glasses to our mouths, taking slow sips so the steam from the hot drink warmed our faces as well as our stomachs. We tried to make the atole last as long as we could, but we had to give our glasses back to the vendor so she could wash them for the next customers. It was a cold morning, and people kept lining up in front of her metal pots.

What to do next? I knew a stall where my mother bought onions and tomatoes. Lucia said we should go there and ask the vendor if she knew any kaxlan ladies who needed a maid. I didn't know exactly where the stall was, but I remembered that the vendor was from Chamula and had a gold tooth that shone brightly when she smiled. So we went looking for a woman in a blue shawl with a gold tooth.

We found her in her stall with two girls about our age. The three were busy selling to a crowd of ladies. After the crowd moved on, one of the girls sat down by a charcoal fire and warmed her hands over the red coals. I wanted to ask if we could join her, but Lucia beat me to it.

"Do you mind if we warm our hands a little? We're really cold."

"I don't mind," the girl said.

Lucia motioned me to come closer. I didn't waste any time squatting next to her and stretching my hands over the coals.

"Where are you from?" the girl asked.

"Lokan, Chenalhó," Lucia answered.

"Where are your parents?"

"At home."

"Ah, your parents let you come to the city without them? How old are you?'

"I'm fourteen. We want to go to middle school, and our parents don't have money to send us. We came here to find work so we can pay for school by ourselves. Once we find work we'll tell our parents."

"And the other girl? Is she your sister?"

"No, we're best friends from school. I'm Lucia and she's Magdalena. What's your name?"

"Esperanza."

"Where do you live?"

"I live at the edge of the city. I used to live in Chamula, but we had to leave and come here."

"Do you like it here?"

"Not as much as Chamula. I miss my sheep. But I'm getting used to it here."

We sat and warmed our hands for a while until I surprised myself when a flood of words came out of my mouth about how we didn't know where to find work and did Esperanza's mother know a couple of kaxlan ladies who needed a maid? I said we knew how to cook, wash clothes, clean the house, and take care of children and many other things and also we spoke a little castellano, especially Lucia who spoke it well.

The girl's sister must have heard my explosion of words because she came over and asked if we were friends from school. Esperanza explained who we were and that we were looking for work. That caught her mother's attention, and she called over from the other side of the stall.

"The señora who just left, the one in the brown shawl with the cane, she might need a servant. Yesterday her maid left to get married. She's over there, looking at some lillies. Go ask her."

Lucia leapt up and ran to the flower vendor's stall where the woman was paying for her flowers. I followed as soon as I realized that Lucia had gone. When I got close to the señora, her back was to me. Her black hair was streaked with grey and wound up in a big coil. When she turned, I saw her face. It looked much kinder than I expected. The wrinkes in the corners of her eyes spread out like rays of sunshine when she smiled. Still, I was afraid to speak, but as usual Lucia found her words.

"Señora, pardon us, but the Chamula lady over there told us that you might need a maid. My friend and I know how to work hard. We can clean, wash, cook, and anything else you need us to do. We only ask for a few hours off to go to school. You see, we want to have different lives from our mothers."

The señora looked surprised, but she was smiling at us. Finally, she said, "Well, well. I see from your blouses that you are girls from Chenalhó, and at least one of you speaks castellano. So you are looking for work? It's true my maid just left, and I do need another one, but I don't need two."

"We understand, señora. But maybe you have a neighbor or a relative who needs a maid?"

"I don't think so. At least I haven't heard that anyone is looking for help."

We hadn't talked about what we would do if it happened that we found only one job. We hadn't planned anything, really. So here we were with the possibility of a job for Lucia, but not one for me. Lucia's mind seemed to be racing ahead trying to figure out what to do, while I just stood by her side not knowing what fate held for me.

"Señora, I would like to work for you if you'll have me, but I need to help my friend find a job too. If you want me to start today, I just need a little time to find work for her. After you're done shopping, we can follow you home, and then go ask the señoras in your neighborhood if they need a girl to work for them. That way, my friend and I will live close to each other."

Our luck finding one job gave Lucia faith that it would hold out long enough to find another. I wasn't so sure, but as usual I trusted Lucia. Still, I didn't like that she took the job so fast without talking to me first.

The señora told us that we looked like girls she could trust and that she would like Lucia to be her maid. Then she said that she had a couple more things to buy, so we trailed behind her until her last stop circled us back near Esperanza's mother's stall. Lucia ran over to tell Esperanza's mother the news about her job and thanked her for her help. Then she motioned for me to follow the señora. I looked longingly at Esperanza and her sister hunched over the coals. I wanted to stay with them and warm myself, but my future was like a living thing running off without me, and I had to catch up.

On the way to the señora's house, Lucia carried the basket of vegetables while we walked single file along the narrow stone sidewalk. We were getting further and further from the market and had no idea where we were. The houses in the señora's neighborhood were connected by tall walls. It was hard to know when one house began and the other ended. A few branches of purple bouganvilla climbed over the walls. We wondered what else filled the patios on the other side of those walls. Were they full of flowers and fruit trees? Were there vegetable gardens, chickens, and turkeys in the backyards?

When we finally arrived at the señora's door, she took a big key from around her neck and unlocked the door. We never locked our doors, so this was something new for us. We waited patiently until the door creaked open. The señora turned around and said, "Come into the kitchen, girls."

To get to the kitchen, we had to walk through a patio full of bouganvilla, rose bushes, and flowering fruit trees with a tank of water in the center and benches along the walls. In the kitchen, the first thing that caught my eye was a big white refrigerator. I'd seen them in Chenalhó. From the gate outside Doña Ermita's bakery, I'd crane my neck to see her refrigerator and imagine what might be inside—heaping plates of candies, cream, cheese, and bottles of sweet milk.

The señora told us to sit down at her table. Then she explained what would happen for the rest of the day. But first she asked us our names and told us hers.

"My name is Dolores… (I don't remember her last names.) Then she said, 'You may call me Doña Dolores. Lucia, later I'll tell you about your work here. Right now it's best for you to look for a job for Magdalena. When you talk to the señoras, explain that you are my new servant. That might help. But I want you back in two hours to help me prepare dinner. It's noon right now. Be back by 2. After dinner I'll show you where you'll sleep, and later we'll talk about letting your parents know where you are. Do you need a glass of water before you go? In the cupboard are some glasses."

The glasses were lined up in neat rows on the bottom shelf. We picked a couple that weren't too big, filled them with water from a pottery jug, and gulped the water down.

We had to be back in two hours. We knocked on one door after another until we were far from Doña Dolores' house, and my feet were aching. At every house we were rejected. Sometimes a maid came to the door and told us the señora didn't need help. Other times a child opened the door and went to get her mother who finally came to tell us she didn't need a servant.

One señora looked us over like we were a couple of pigs she was thinking about buying and then closed the door before we had a chance to say we were sorry to bother her. One señora was very kind and recommended some houses that might need help. But no one needed a servant.

Before our time was up, I had my fill of rejection.

I was really worried as we headed back to Doña Dolores' house. Where was I going to stay that night if we didn't find work for me? Would Doña Dolores let me stay in her house with Lucia? With my head full of worry we knocked on Doña Dolores' door.

Doña Dolores didn't seem surprised that we hadn't found work. She told us that after we ate we could go back out and try again. She put us to work chopping vegetables that she had washed and laid out on the counter. There were little red potatoes, chayotes, carrots, onions, tomatoes, and chiles. And a chicken was cooking on the stove. I could smell it when we came in, and the thought of eating chicken made me forget my worry. While the soup was cooking, Doña Dolores showed us Lucia's room on one side of the patio. It had a bed, a table, and a clothes cupboard. There were burlap bags with something in them stacked in the corner. Doña Dolores gave us two clean sheets to put on the bed and told us to make the bed while she finished the meal. We had never slept in sheets or on a bed with a mattress. I helped Lucia lay the smooth sheet over the mattress and then another one on top of it. We figured out that must be how it's done. I asked Lucia if she thought Doña Dolores would let me sleep in the bed with her that night. Lucia told me that even if we found a job for me, she would ask the señora if I could stay in her room that night, so we could talk about what we would say to our parents when they came looking for us.

After we finished making the bed we returned to the kitchen and found Doña Dolores already eating and reading a book at the same time. We'd never seen anyone do that. Later that evening Lucia told me that it was a good sign that Doña Dolores liked to read because she would probably keep her promise about letting her go to school. We looked longingly at Doña Dolores' bowl of soup. We'd had nothing to eat except a few toasted tortillas and our stomachs were rumbling. She told us to serve ourselves some soup and sit down with her. The soup was delicious. The tortillas from the tortillera weren't as good as the ones our mothers made but they filled our stomachs. The señora asked us some questions about our famiies and told us a little about herself, how she had been a teacher and never married. Then she laid down her napkin and said, "Well, girls, I'm going to take a nap now. You can go out and look for work when you're ready. Go in the other direction this time and be sure to come back before it's dark so you won't get lost. Lucia, when you come back we'll talk about your terms of employment and how to inform your parents."

Walking the other way wasn't any better. Nobody wanted a servant girl. When it was starting to get dark and we turned a corner that opened up a whole new street, instead of feeling hopeful, I felt that my dream of finding a job and going to school would never come true.

I tugged on Lucia's shawl and told her, "I don't want to knock on another door. We're not going to find a job for me. It's good enough that you have a job. If one of us goes to school, it's better than neither of us.

I'm going home tomorrow. I'll beg my parents pardon, and ask them to tell your mother where you are. She'll come to visit, and she'll see the good food the señora gives you and that she agrees for you to go to school. It'll be alright."

Lucia stood very still. I did too. In that moment I think we both saw that our lives were soon to be like a forked path. Still, Lucia tried to convince me to keep looking for work.

"Let's keep looking for a job for you so you can have the same chances I have. Let's not give up. It's too early to give up."

"I'm not as brave as you," I said. "I'm embarrassed to knock on doors and talk to strangers. It's sad to give up my dream and go back to Lokan, but when you come to visit, you can tell me all about your life in the city, and it will be almost like I'm here. And when I come to visit, you'll show me all the places you know and what you're learning in school. We'll still be friends."

Lucia could see that I had made up my mind, and so we turned around and returned to Doña Dolores' house. The señora let us in and told us to join her by the fireplace where she had been sitting. Once we were seated on little stools by the fire, she asked us, "Did you have any luck, girls?"

"No, Doña Dolores, we couldn't find work for Magdalena. We don't think it's easy to find another job."

Doña Dolores put her book down and looked a little sad. "I was afraid you might not find a job for Magdalena that easily. I'm sorry about that. But God worked one miracle for us today, and that's probably more than we deserve. It's best that you return to your parents in the morning, Magdalena. They must be worried about you, and Lucia's parents need to know where she is. Perhaps you can return another day to look for a job if your parents give you permission. Tonight you may sleep in Lucia's room with her. There's a petate you can use, and I have lots of blankets."

"Thank you, Doña Dolores," Lucia said, "but Magdalena and I can sleep together in my bed. We just need another blanket."

Before we said goodnight, Doña Dolores told Lucia that her responsibilities would be to go to market each morning, to prepare the midday meal, and to wash the dishes after. She would also feed the chickens, mop the floors, and wash the señora's clothes when they were dirty. In return, Doña Dolores would pay Lucia thirty pesos a month, more than most servants made back then.

After a month, if Lucia had shown that she was a good worker and committed to doing her best in school, Doña Dolores would enroll her in middle school and pay her school expenses. In the meantime Lucia could read any of Doña Dolores' books she wanted.

We were so tired that we hardly talked at all before we fell asleep in Lucia's bed. We knew there was nothing we could do but hope that my parents wouldn't punish me too hard and that Lucia's mother would agree to her working for Doña Dolores. Before I started to drift off to sleep, Lucia tried to comfort me by saying that she would keep looking for a job for me, and that, if she found one, we would convince my parents to let me live in the city and study.

The next day was very hard for me, and for my parents and Lucia too. I don't like to remember it, but I'll tell you what you need to know.

After breakfast Doña Dolores sent us to the market to buy vegetables. We went to Esperanza's mother's stall first. Esperanza saw us coming and ran toward me to tell me that my parents had come looking for us. They came to her mother's stall early that morning and asked if she had seen two girls from Chenalhó. She thought they might be looking for us and asked Esperanza our names. My father said that if we came to buy something to be sure to keep us there. Then my parents left and said they'd be back to see if we had come. I asked Esperanza how my parents looked, and she said my father looked angry and my mother was crying.

I didn't have any choice but to stay and wait for my parents. Lucia went back to Doña Dolores' house with the vegetables and said she'd wait there for me and my parents. So, I waited, scared and alone. Esperanza tried to cheer me up by talking non-stop about whatever came into her head.

It wasn't long before I saw my father's face in the crowd of shoppers. Behind him was my mother, her face smeared with tears. They came hurriedly toward me. My father grabbed me by the arm and started to yell at me. I don't remember what he said. I just remember how ashamed and scared I felt while his words fell down on me. My mother stood behind him crying while my father scolded me harder than I'd ever been scolded in my life. I thought that if this wasn't my punishment, I didn't know how I could bear a harder one. I was scared that maybe my father was waiting to hit me when we got home.

Still holding my arm, my father thanked Esperanza's mother and told me to take them to where Lucia was. On the way to Doña Dolores' house, I explained that Lucia had a job as a maid, but that I didn't have one, and that I was planning to go home on the next bus. That information didn't calm my father's anger.

When we finally got to Doña Dolores' door, I thought Lucia would answer it, but she was hiding in her room afraid of what my parents would say. Doña Dolores opened the door and asked my parents to come in. Lucia had told her that my parents had come for me, so Doña Dolores had a little talk prepared for when they arrived. I remember her words well because they calmed my father down, and I learned that Doña Dolores had wanted to go to school like me when she was a girl.

"I can only imagine how scared you were when Magdalena didn't come home last night. I'm glad that now you're reunited with your daughter. She was planning to return home today and apologize to you for running away. Now that you've come, please sit down so we can discuss how to handle the problem of Lucia wanting to stay here with me to work and study."

My parents had calmed down a little by then. They accepted Doña Dolores' offer to sit with her on a bench in her patio. There she explained to them that long ago she had gone to school in Mexico City where she had learned to be a teacher. She understood how Lucia and I felt because she too had had a dream to study as far as she could. With her parents' and God's help she was able to.

After she returned to San Cristóbal, she taught for many years and was proud of her students who went on to become teachers like her—or sometimes secretaries or nurses. She had never married and over the years had helped several of her maids go to school. They became like her daughters and most of them still visited her. It was a blessing, she said, when she met us in the market because she was very worried how she would go on without her maid who had just left.

My parents listened to Doña Dolores, and then my father said respectfully but sternly, "We understand that you want to help Lucia and that you have cared for her and our daughter until we could come for them. We'd like to talk to Lucia now so we can be sure she wants to stay with you. Then we'll talk to her mother, and she'll come here and talk with you."

Doña Dolores called for Lucia who came out of her room and stood next to me while my father asked her if she really wanted to stay and work for Doña Dolores and keep studying. Lucia looked at the ground while my father talked, but when he had finished she looked him in the face and told him that she wanted to study more than anything in the world, that she was very sorry that she had made him have to come to the city to find us, but she would work and study hard and make us all proud of her. She said that after studying she would find a job and help her mother and others in our community with her earnings.

That was the end of my San Cristóbal adventure. I gathered up my things, thanked Doña Dolores for giving me a place to sleep and tried not to cry when I said goodbye to Lucia. I remember walking out the door with my parents. I felt there was nothing left to look forward to in my life.

My father didn't hit me when we got home. I think he could tell that I was too ashamed to ever lie to them or hurt them again. And I never did. Our lives just continued as if I had never run away. Except at night, after my parents were asleep, I would cry, thinking about how my life could have been if I had stayed in San Cristóbal.

My mother still had to talk to Lucia's mother. Carmela was relieved to know where Lucia was and that she had found a place to work and that she would also be able to study. As soon as she could, Carmela went to San Cristóbal to see Lucia. Doña Dolores must have given the same speech to Carmela because when she came back, she stopped by our house to tell my mother what had happened. She said that it must be God's will that her daughter found work with such a kind señora who would help her go to school. Carmela said she would miss her daughter, but she would manage with Hilario's help. She asked me if I'd like to go with her the next time she went to visit Lucia. I said yes, of course. It had only been a few days, and already I missed Lucia.

"COME, HILARIO, COME."

FOR A FEW DAYS, I couldn't talk into the tape recorder about Lucia because Victorio and I had to go to a course that the madres organized in Yabteclum. I left Verónica at home to take care of our store. Although we were only gone two days, I knew she would be anxious for me to return and continue Lucia's story.

After the course had finished and we climbed out of the truck that brought us home, I looked up the hill and there was Verónica standing on a rock below our house watching the road. She hadn't done that since she was a little girl waiting for us to come home from a meeting and rescue her from her brothers, who ordered her around and wouldn't play with her.

Sometimes when I came home, I'd find her weaving on a toy loom that she'd made out of sticks she found on the ground. Her loom would be tied to a low tree branch and there she would be, pretending to weave with my stray threads. When she saw me, she'd jump up and proudly hold her creation up for me to inspect. I'd look it over and say, "That's good. Continue with that."

The morning after I returned from Yabteclum, I told Verónica I could talk about Lucia again. To get me started, Verónica asked how life was for Carmela and Hilario without Lucia.

With Lucia living in San Cristóbal, Hilario didn't have a helper when he went to heal. After she had been gone a couple weeks, he came to our house to heal my brother, who had a terrible stomach ache. Hilario knelt on the ground with difficulty and prayed so softly I could hardly hear him.

The next morning after breakfast, my mother wrapped a few eggs in a striped tortilla cloth and said she was going to visit Carmela. She told me to stay and watch my little sister Ernestina, who, by that time, was almost ready to go to school but was still too little to be left alone.

Ernestina was very naughty when she was little. Once my father got so angry at her for screaming at the top of her lungs when my mother wouldn't give her more atole that he spanked her hard and yelled at my mother. The rest of the day my father stayed outside the house making a net bag and not talking to anyone. In the evening he came back to the house with some branches and asked my mother to boil a pot of water. He put the branches in the water and let them simmer. Then mother went to get Ernestina and told her they were going to do a special prayer for her. Ernestina liked the attention from my parents and didn't fight them when they took off her clothes and bathed her in the water from the boiled branches. Afterwards, they wrapped her in my mother's shawl and held her between them while they said a prayer that my father told me later is called "to the mother, to the father."

"Forgive me, what I did to you.
I didn't know what I was doing to you,
because I was angry.
Perhaps resentment made me do it."

After praying, my father told me that when his parents had argued or scolded him unfairly they would bathe him and pray, and he would never get sick from their anger. Our parents and grandparents believed that a parent's anger could make a child sick, even an adult child. After praying to ask forgiveness, the parents would drink a cup of pox, but since my father no longer drank he left out that part.

The prayer worked for the rest of the day with Ernestina, but the next day she went back to her bad ways. Maybe the prayer helped in the end, though, because today she's a respectful woman. I wish we saw her more often, but that's how it is after women marry and go to live in their husband's community.

When Mother came back from visiting Carmela, she told me that Hilario was very sick and that he wanted Lucia at home to pray for him. Carmela was going to go to San Cristóbal the next day to bring her home, just for a few days. I was very excited to see Lucia again.

Lucia returned with her mother to Lokan the next day. It was exactly one month since we had run away and the end of her month of proving to Doña Dolores that she deserved to go to school. When I went with my family to Lucia's house, I waited while she finished praying for Hilario. Carmela told us that Lucia had been praying for him continuously since she returned.

About a dozen Believers arrived before us. They knelt beside rows of candles that had been placed on the ground outside the door of the house where Lucia was praying. Hilario had healed practically everyone in the community at one time or another. Over the coming days, they came to visit him. They brought tortillas, beans, sodas, pox, coffee, rolls, and firewood. The stack of firewood outside Carmela's door grew so big that it extended several yards into the patio. I had never seen so much firewood in one place!

My mother and I helped Carmela make coffee and tortillas and beans to give to the visitors. My brother handed out pox to those who drank and sodas for the Believers. That night our family and some of the other Believers stayed and slept on petates on the kitchen floor. I waited for Lucia to come into the kitchen to sleep. I wanted so much to see her and ask about her new life in San Cristóbal.

I was lying on my petate getting sleepy when Lucia finally opened the kitchen door. Her mother gave her a gourd of matz, and Lucia drank it down quickly. Carmela said there was still chicken soup if Lucia wanted some, but she only wanted to sleep. I pulled my blanket aside, and Lucia slipped in beside me. I put my arms around her and told her how happy I was to see her. She smiled and rested her head on my shoulder.

"Until tomorrow," she whispered before she fell asleep.

In the morning Hilario woke up feeling a little better. Everyone was happy. Soon people started to roll up their petates and pack their things to go back home. It seemed that the crisis had past. After breakfast Lucia and I went to fetch water at the water hole. We talked all the way there and back and rested on the path just to have more time to talk. I asked her if she ate chicken every day at Doña Dolores' house.

"No, but we eat well. Sometimes we have fish or beef. I wanted to save some of the food for you, but it would have spoiled before we saw each other."

"That's alright. You know how it is here—we're not starving. How about your work? Did Doña Dolores work you hard?"

"No, I didn't have to work that hard. Her clothes didn't get that dirty so I didn't have to wash often. I went to the market every morning, but I really liked that. I learned to cook a lot of things.

"On Sunday evening, Doña Dolores asked me to walk with her to the center of the city to listen to miramba music. We would sit on a bench in the park and watch the people. The mestizos have this custom where boys walk one way around the zocalo and the girls walk the other, and they get to look at each other and pick out someone they like. The girls dress up in their prettiest clothes, and the boys slick their hair back to look handsome.

"It's so different from our tradition where we can't talk to boys until we marry. That got me thinking that our tradition isn't fair. I don't want to wait for a man to ask my parents to marry me. I don't think I even want to marry. Once I have a job I can support myself and won't need a husband. In fact, if he drank or ordered me around the way men do, he might just make my life harder."

I was thinking about what Lucia said because I hadn't thought of not marrying. In fact since my plan to go to school failed, I'd been praying to God to send me a good man like my father who didn't drink, helped my mother, and listened to the word of God. I just didn't want him to come too soon, though, before I was ready to get married. I couldn't imagine life without a companion and children to help me when I grow old, just like you and your brothers are doing for me now.

I told Lucia my thoughts and she said, "Sometimes I wish that I felt like you because I might be lonely without a companion, and when I get a job it probably won't be in Lokan. That will mean I'll have to get to know strangers and their ways. They might not even speak our language!

I hope the women will be like Doña Dolores and the men will be like—I don't know, maybe like your father?"

We had to get back to the house with the water, so we got up from the rock where we'd been sitting and ran the rest of the way down the trail. Lucia hadn't forgotten how to run downhill with two pails of water. She belonged in Lokan. How could she not see this? I was thinking these thoughts because I was jealous. I didn't want it to be true that Lucia had a job and would soon be going to school.

In the following days Lucia and I visited often. She wanted to go back to San Cristóbal to start school but didn't want to leave her grandfather until she was sure he was strong again. I think she might have felt that by running away she had abandoned her grandfather who depended on her to help him in his work as a healer.

But then something happened that we didn't expect. One morning when Hilario didn't come into the kitchen to drink his matz, Lucia went to see how he was. He was still in bed with his eyes closed, but he wasn't sleeping. He had died in the night.

As soon as I found out the sad news, I ran to Lucia's house. I sat with Lucia beside Hilario's body for three days while almost everyone in Lokan came to say goodbye to him. After they entered the house, they knelt before Carmela and told her how sorry they were that Hilario had died. Lucia only left Hilario's side to bring food to the mourners or to give mashed tortillas to a kitten sleeping by the fire. Everyone just ate, prayed, and wept as the days passed. Even my father wept.

My father was in charge of making sure that we carried out all the rituals correctly. Although he was a Believer, he respected the traditions too and hadn't forgotten what the ancestors wanted us to do when people die. The ancestors say that one's body is planted in the earth like a tree and needs help to uproot itself.

When it was time to take Hilario's body out of the house, my father motioned for the men to lift his pine box off the boards where it rested. Then Mol Miguel, a healer who was a little younger than Hilario, laid the boards against the wall of the house and whipped them hard with a leather strap, all the while saying, "I'm punishing you so that you don't become accustomed to holding the bodies of dead people, so that you don't let demons enter you. Get out of these boards, demons. Leave this house in peace. Let all illness leave this house."

At that moment, the bodies of the mourners became like one. Those at the front tried to step out the door, but those behind pulled them back. Our hearts wanted to keep Hilario there with us, but we had to let him go, the man who had done so much good for us.

My father chose two elderly couples to stay in Hilario's house after we carried him to the cemetery. Their work was to sweep the house clean of evil spirits and sprinkle chiles on the ground to purify it.

Mol Miguel led the procession to the cemetery carrying a gourd of water with three marigolds. He called to Hilario, "Come, Hilario, come. We're leaving this house. We're going to find another house. Your soul is leaving. Let's go."

Mol Humberto, another elder, followed Hilario's coffin with a basket of money for Hilario to carry with him to Heaven. The men had a discussion about how much money Hilario should take with him. They didn't want to give him too much to carry, because Hilario was a humble man who never had much money when he lived. But they didn't want Hilario to go with too little, because he was a man of great value to his people.

They settled on a hundred pesos which was quite a bit of money at that time. My father had taken up a collection among all the families.

The men carried Hilario down the mountain through the cornfields to the cemetery. Lucia was at the front of the procession behind her mother. I followed behind my parents in a long column of people. Lucia wasn't as tall as the corn that came right up to the sides of the trail, so I lost sight of her until we arrived at the cemetery.

All the graves in the cemetery were covered with soul houses made with roofs of thatch. Even though some men wanted to build a house with a metal roof for Hilario, Carmela wanted him to have a humble soul house like everyone else. She didn't like the metal roofs that were starting to appear in the cemetery. Now most soul houses have metal roofs.

I'm like Carmela though. When I die I want a thatched roof on my soul house, just like the house I was born in.

Please remember that, daughter.

I made my way through the mourners to where Lucia was standing by the grave the men had dug the day before. Although she was looking into the hole, I could see that her face was streaked with tears. I took her hand as the men lowered Hilario's coffin into the hole. Carmela placed his hat, tunic, wool poncho, and two string bags along the sides of his body. Then Mol Miguel placed the gourd of water with three marigolds at the head of the coffin. Finally, my father put the things Hilario used in his prayers in the box: incense, candles, a little bit of pox, and two sticks to defend himself against animals that might bother him on his journey to heaven.

After the men closed the coffin, my mother looked at me, her eyes wide with fear, and said, "Daughter, there are children here whose souls are in danger of being caught up with Hilario. We must show them how to throw dirt on the coffin so their souls won't leave the earth." Mother and I scooped up handfuls of dirt from the mounds surrounding the grave and beckoned the little children to come near the edge of the hole where Hilario lay. We gave each of them handfuls of dirt while Mother explained the purpose of our tradition. After all the children and adults had finished throwing three handfuls of dirt, we knelt and my father led us in prayer.

Soon after the funeral, Carmela came to our house to talk to my mother. I was outside weaving and strained to hear their conversation through the cracks in the wall.

Carmela told my mother something that would change Lucia's life again. "A few days before Hilario died, I heard him praying outside in the middle of the night. I got out of bed and looked through the door, and there he was tying two tree branches together while asking the Earth Lord to tie Lucia's soul to her house and to Lokan, to end her life in San Cristóbal!

"The next morning, I was afraid to ask him directly about his prayer. Instead, I asked him what he thought about Lucia living in San Cristóbal. He was very forceful when he answered me. He said, 'My life is going to end soon, and our community will need Lucia to take my place. She's wasting her powers in San Cristóbal. The kaxlanetik don't respect our traditions and think healers are witches.'"

My mother sat quietly for a few minutes after Carmela spoke.

"I know Hilario did much good for our people, but you can't deny that when he prayed to the Earth Lord he did exactly what the kaxlanetik say that witches do. He tried to control another's destiny."

Carmela nodded because it was true what my mother said, even though she didn't want to disrespect Hilario's memory. My mother moved the logs further into the fire and waited for Carmela to say something. Finally, Carmela asked my mother, "Should I tell Lucia that Hilario wants her to return to Lokan, to be his replacement? Do you think that God will punish me for cutting off my daughter's dream of an education?"

"Only God knows what fate holds for each person," my mother told her. Then she said, "Let's pray about this."

And so they got down on their knees, pulled their shawls over their heads, and prayed. I sat quietly until their prayer ended. My heart was a tangle of thoughts. I didn't want Lucia to lose her dream because it felt almost like my own. But I also wanted her back in Lokan so we could help one another through all the things to come in our lives.

MY DAUGHTER'S SORROW

IT WAS MY TURN at the Zapatista co-op store for a month, so Verónica and I took a break from talking about Lucia's story. When it's my turn at the co-op store, I enjoy being in a different place for a while. I keep busy straightening the cans on the shelves and hanging the weaving threads. When my compañeras need to buy something or stop to say hello on their way home from the fields, I hear all the latest gossip.

The co-op store is just above Lucia's house. During the first year of the store, Lucia would keep me company. In between customers, we'd talk while we embroidered. Even now after she's been gone so long, I hear her calling to me as she climbs the trail, "Vishin! Sister!"

But then I look outside, and there's no one there.

When I came home each evening after working at the co-op store, Verónica stayed in the sleeping house working on her weaving and watching TV. I knew she was angry about something, probably being left alone to take care of our own store.

One evening I asked her what was wrong. She poured out a lot of anger and pain that she had kept inside her. Her words cut into my heart and made me remember how she suffered last year after she left school to marry Rodrigo.

When it was her time to graduate from primary school, Verónica begged us to let her attend the middle school in the lum. After much discussion, Victorio and I relented. But we told her she would have to make some money selling her weavings to pay for her school expenses since we couldn't afford to pay them. She was already selling her weavings so she was confident she could find the money she needed. We also told her that each day at school she would have to study hard and not look for boyfriends.

But it was impossible for her not to think of boys! One day, a few weeks after she started middle school, she was walking home and passed by the place where the taxi drivers park their cars. Rodrigo saw her and started to talk to her. Soon they began to walk around town holding hands. Her brothers, Abolino and Sebastian, knew Rodrigo and the other taxi drivers. When they saw Rodrigo with Verónica, they came right home to tell us that their sister wasn't obeying us.

Victorio and I didn't understand how it is to go to middle school in the lum, how it's possible to study and also have a boyfriend. We only knew what we heard and were afraid that Verónica might get pregnant and then have to marry without the proper respect that comes with doing joyol, the traditional bride petition. So we told Verónica that she had to choose— stay in school and stop looking for boyfriends—or marry Rodrigo.

If we had only let her be Rodrigo's girlfriend, she would have learned that he wasn't a good person, and then she wouldn't have married him. But she chose to leave school and marry him, and then it was too late.

Only a couple months after she went to live with Rodrigo, we had to rescue her and bring her home. One day when they were talking with the other taxi drivers, Abolino and Sebastian overheard Rodrigo boasting that he could make his wife do anything he wanted. He just had to beat her if she refused. My sons came home to tell us what they'd heard. Immediately we prepared to go to Rodrigo's community to bring our daughter home. Even though her brothers had informed on their sister, forcing us to make her choose between Rodrigo and school, in the end they saved her life.

I'll never forget how I felt when we got out of the taxi in Baxilum. I was afraid of Rodrigo from what I had heard about him, and I didn't know what his parents were like. I didn't know if we would see them or if Lucia would be home alone or if we could just take her home with us and then deal with Rodrigo and his parents later.

"We need to ask someone where Rodrigo's parents live," I said to Victorio after we got out of the car.

"All right, let's go to the store across the road and ask there."

The storekeeper told us where their house was, but he said that Rodrigo didn't live there, that Rodrigo and his new wife lived in a little house not far up the road because his parents already had two daughters-in-law living with them.

That information worried me, because it meant that no one was there to stop Rodrigo from beating our daughter. I started to walk faster and told Victorio we needed to hurry. Soon we found the house and Victorio called from the door for Verónica.

"Daughter, are you there?"

At first no one answered, but then we heard Verónica tell us to come in. It took some time to adjust my eyes to the darkness of the kitchen, so at first I only saw the outline of Verónica sitting by the fire. Gradually, the damage done to her was revealed to me, as if I were slowly taking a blanket off a person who had been in a serious accident. My poor daughter's face was covered with bruises. One eye was half shut and black bruises covered her other eye and cheekbones. Her lips were bruised too, and blood was caked in the corners of her mouth. She was as thin as our poor dog.

Victorio held my elbow as we came close to Verónica. I sat down and put my arms around her. She clung to me and sobbed, "Please, Mother, take me home."

"Oh, daughter, forgive us for what we let happen to you!"

"Daughter, we need to leave now. Where are your things?" Victorio asked.

"Under the bed in a box, Father. I don't have much. Please don't forget my loom, it's standing by the door. And the comal is ours too."

We gathered up all of Verónica's things and hurried out the door to find a car back to Lokan. There was no one in the road while we waited. Probably some people watched us from their houses. I wonder what they thought. Perhaps they knew what had happened in that house, as I'm sure Verónica cried out for help when Rodrigo hit her. I wish she had gone to them for help. They could have gotten word to us.

Once we were inside the car, Verónica covered her face with her shawl and leaned her head against the window.

"Thank God, Verónica isn't pregnant," I said to Victorio that night.

"Yes, in time she may be able to marry again."

I watched Verónica closely for a few months and nothing changed, so at least she could marry again, if she wanted to. Although things are changing, many men still don't want to marry a woman with a child from another man.

It only took a few weeks for Verónica's bruises to disappear, but it took much longer for her sadness to pass. I encouraged her to weave. She said she had barely touched her loom when she lived with Rodrigo. I think it helped her to weave and do other things she enjoyed, like singing in the church choir. But she rarely laughed or joked anymore. Her soul had been badly treated and it needed time to come back to her.

I tried to be patient with her. Sometimes Victorio wasn't as understanding as I wished he would be. He suffered a lot when we had to go talk to Rodrigo's parents and tell them how their son had mistreated our daughter. They didn't protest our right to take her home and never brought up the matter of returning the money that Rodrigo paid in place of living with us and working with Victorio.

But they didn't admit to us what a bad son they had raised, and they never apologized to us. Victorio was very angry on the way back to Lokan and stayed that way for a while. I had to remind him that sometimes protecting a daughter's soul means being disrespected in ways we could never imagine.

By harvest time, Verónica had almost recovered and seemed like her old self again. But some evenings sitting around the fire, she still looked sad. I think she was wondering about her future and was worried. I kept wishing I had stood up for my daughter's right to go to school, even if it meant having a boyfriend. But there was no going back.

One day I was in the lum shopping, and I stopped at the door of the Casa de La Cultura. Something on the door caught my attention. It was an announcement in big letters about a project hiring young women to interview older women about their lives. I borrowed a pen from a man sitting at a desk inside the doorway and wrote the telephone number of the office in San Cristóbal on the palm of my hand.

When I got home, I told Verónica about the job and gave her the number. Then I forgot about it for the rest of the day. But Verónica didn't forget. The next morning she was up before me and off to make a call at the house of our neighbor who had a phone. I watched with pleasure as she trotted down the road below our house, her braids blowing in the wind.

When Verónica returned, she told me that they were interviewing girls in the lum the next day, and she wanted to apply.

"I think you have a good chance of getting the job, daughter. You're intelligent and hard working."

"I hope so, Mother. I want to do something in my life, be something more than a mother and housewife. I don't mean to disrespect you, but you know I've always wanted to study and have a job."

"I don't feel disrespected. I accept who I am."

The next day Verónica went back to the lum for her interview. She must have impressed Diana, the director, because she got the job. She came home in the afternoon swinging a bag of papers the organization had given her and telling me it was time to celebrate! I bought her a bottle of cherry soda, her favorite soft drink, and we sat together in our store listening to Zapatista ballads on the radio. Although Verónica has had days of sadness since, I think her soul has finally returned.

LUCIA CHOOSES

THE DAY AFTER I FINISHED my turn at the Zapatista co-op store, Verónica and I continued talking about Lucia. We stayed by the fire because a fine drizzle made everything damp and chilly. Our neighbors must have had the same idea to stay inside because the only person who came to the store was a neighbor who needed candles. As always happened when I started talking, I remembered things I hadn't thought of in a long time. I began after Carmela told Lucia about Hilario's wishes before he died.

Even before Lucia heard what her grandfather had wanted, her heart was divided between living in the city and staying with her mother in Lokan. I came to visit her the day she finally decided to stay in Lokan. She was in the patio sitting on a wood block embroidering a tortilla cloth.

When she saw me, she wiped her eyes with her shawl. She'd been crying. I didn't know what to say to lift her spirits, so I just sat beside her and helped her take kernels off a pile of corncobs. As the kernels from the last cob fell into the basket, she said, "I need to tell Doña Dolores that I'm not coming back to San Cristóbal."

"Are you sure that you don't want to go to school?" I asked her.

"Yes, I'm sure. Mother said it was my choice, but I can't abandon her. If I go back to San Cristóbal, she'll have to work all alone in the house and fields and eat and sleep alone. Her heart will be so sad. When I ran away to go to school, I didn't think about my mother because

Hilario was still alive. I also didn't want to think about the cargo that the Moon Virgin gave me. She put it inside my heart, but I've kept it there without using it for more than a month. If I go back to San Cristóbal, it will just stay inside me and do no good for anyone. It might even hurt me or someone else. Please help me, Magdalena. I have to write a letter to Doña Dolores and tell her that I'm not coming back."

Lucia found an old notebook and tore out a piece of paper. It took us a long time to write the letter, because each word felt like a post in a corral that we were building to keep Lucia inside. When we finished, she read the letter out loud. As I remember, it said:

Very esteemed Doña Dolores,

I write you with very bad news for me and for you. After I returned to Lokan, my grandfather died. He was a healer and he taught me to heal too. It was his last wish that I carry on his work. So I have to stay and serve my cargo. Please pardon me for leaving you without a servant. You were very kind to me when I lived with you, and you taught me many things, like how to cook different food. I also learned many things from the books in your library. God knows that I wanted to go to school when I returned to San Cristóbal, but it wasn't His will. May He find you another helper very soon.

Your devoted servant for one month,

Lucia signed her letter with her special signature that looked like a vine curling around itself sprouting blossoms here and there. We learned how to make our signatures in school. I struggled to make mine, but Lucia learned fast and enjoyed writing her signature whenever she had a chance. If I saw it again, I would recognize it right away, and Lucia's spirit would fill me.

My brother was going to San Cristóbal and offered to deliver the letter to Doña Dolores. When Ricardo returned from his trip, he brought a letter from Doña Dolores for Lucia. Ricardo and I took it to Lucia, and we read it together.

Doña Dolores started her letter with, "My very dear Lucia," and ended it, "With much affection, Dolores." I still can't remember her last names! Her letter was short, but it left an impression on us. We had never received a letter from a kaxlan lady.

In her letter, Doña Dolores said that she was very sorry that Hilario had died and understood why Lucia needed to stay in Lokan. Then she told Lucia something that I've never forgotten because I saw Lucia struggle so hard to do what Doña Dolores wanted her to. Doña Dolores wrote that although Lucia's plans for school didn't come to pass, she hoped that Lucia would have the courage to stay close to the way she was made.

Lucia and I had never thought about how we were made. We just thought that our parents had made us, and our work was to be like them and follow what the ancestors told us to do. Later when we started listening to the word of God, we learned that we were made in God's image. That was confusing at first, because we also learned that we were God's children, so how could we be both like God and his children? These were some of the confusions we confronted when we started listening to the word of God.

Lucia and I began to talk about these things after we started going to courses that the madres from the diocese held in Yabteclum. The nuns had a house there where they would stay for a few days at a time, so they could gather us together, the women and girls who were learning about the word of God. Lucia and I went and when our mothers could get away from their work, they went too.

Carmela said that it was important for Lucia to learn the Catholic prayers because Hilario always said that our people need all the help they can get. Carmela took Hilario's words to mean that every prayer is valuable. My parents were happy that I wanted to go to the courses so I could learn the songs and prayers and make the world like God intended it to be.

I've forgotten most of the courses, but I remember one well, because that day we met Madre Ester, a young nun from Mexico City who became very important to us, especially to Lucia.

Lucia and I left for the course about 4 a.m. We took the trails that wound through the forest from Lokan to Yabteclum because it was faster than the road. We carried sticks of pitch pine to light the way. We didn't have flashlights back then.

I wasn't accustomed to walking on the trails in the dark, but by that time Lucia had become familiar with most of the trails for many miles around our community through her work as a healer. It was as if her feet were her eyes. She never lost her footing on the rocky sections of the trail and caught me once when I lost mine on a slippery rock.

When the first light fell through the tall pines we came to a place where not only the path but the whole land was pure rocks with just a little bit of soil in between. I don't know how the people there could survive on that land. But to my amazement, the hillside was scattered with hundreds of squash plants, bigger than any squash I'd seen in the fields of Lokan. Corn grew there too. It stood tall between the rocks, and ropes of beans covered the hillside like garlands at a fiesta.

After three hours of walking, we arrived tired and hungry at the madres' house.

Verónica, I want to explain why we called the nuns madres instead of sisters. We considered them to be the priests' complements, and since we call the priests padres, we thought it only fair to call the nuns madres. At first Lucia and I wondered if the nuns and priests lived together, like husbands and wives. But later we realized that wasn't possible, because there weren't enough padres to go around. But we always thought it was sad that the padres and madres didn't have partners.

Before Madre Ester, we would often get bored listening to the madres read Bible verses and talk to us. The madres couldn't speak our language very well, but that didn't stop them from trying to read to us from a tsotsil translation of the Bible. While they read to us, I remember staring off into the distance and thinking about the rolls and coffee that we would have at our morning break.

After we had suffered through a couple of courses, Lucia stood up and asked Madre Evangelina if she would like her to read the verses from the Bible. Madre Evangelina handed the Bible to Lucia with an expression of relief. From that time on, Lucia read the verses in tsotsil, and the courses were much more interesting.

Each morning, we stopped after a couple hours to drink coffee and eat rolls that the madres brought from San Cristóbal. This morning we watched as Madre Ester ladled coffee into cups. We didn't drink coffee back then, so we just took our rolls and sat down under an orange tree to eat them. Madre Ester poured herself a cup of coffee. Instead of joining the other madres, she came over to sit with us under the tree while we ate the last of our rolls.

I liked how Madre Ester looked. She was small like us and had black hair too, but it was cut short and ended just below her ears. She smiled a lot. Her face opened up when she did, like a window into her heart. She wore a dark skirt like the madres, with a white blouse and a brown sweater.

"There you are!" she said as she sat down with us. "I'm so happy that you've come. You're Lucia, right? You read Samuel 2:8 so beautifully, especially where it says, 'He raises the poor from the dust and lifts the needy from the ash heap.'"

Then Madre Ester looked at me and asked my name. I realized that ever since she began talking to us, she had been speaking in tsotsil!

Lucia and I looked at each other in amazement and laughed. Madre Ester must have thought we were just being silly girls. Lucia explained that we were so surprised that she spoke our language well.

"How did you learn tsotsil?" Lucia asked.

"When I arrived in Chiapas about a year ago, I decided that I needed to speak tsotsil if I was going to serve God here. I knew that I would never learn tsotsil unless I lived with people who speak it every day. So I asked the Mother Superior if I could live with a tsotsil family. At first she told me that no madre had ever done this before, and she didn't think it was a good idea.

"But she prayed about it and eventually gave me permission to live with the family of a catechist in Venustiano Carranza. In exchange for my food and a place to sleep, I helped Juan's wife and daughters with their housework, and I worked in the fields with Juan too."

Madre Ester explained that after two months of living in Juan's house, she moved to a different family's home and stayed with them for two months. She lived with a new family every two months so that no family would be too greatly envied by the others that didn't have her help.

The Mother Superior agreed to this plan because, as I've told you, envy was a big problem in the past. Madre Ester even stayed in a couple homes of Presbyterians because she wanted them to know that there is only one God, and that He wants us to love one another. I don't think she told the Mother Superior about those visits. She only went back to San Cristóbal a few times that year. One time she was really sick and needed a doctor.

At first it was hard for the families to see that Madre Ester was just a person like them, no more important in God's eyes than they are. She let them call her Madre Ester, but she served her own matz each morning and helped make tortillas for the family. She also washed her own clothes at the water hole and took turns with the women collecting water. At night she would help the children with their homework and talk about the word of God with their parents.

Little by little the neighbors got accustomed to seeing Madre Ester at the water hole. They didn't envy the family she was living with because they had heard that Madre Ester would be going to help another family soon, and they hoped it would be their family. Each day Madre Ester spoke tsotsil from morning until night. She even started to dream in tsotsil! She admitted it was very hard at first. For example, she wasn't accustomed to drinking matz and not being able to bathe often. But she explained that her group of madres ate and lived very simply, so it wasn't that much different living in an indigenous home, except that she laughed a lot more than she did living with the madres.

It was time to go back to the meeting. Madre Ester put her arms through ours as we walked to the classroom. Later when we were ready to go home, she gave us a big hug and said, "Chino riox batel. May God go with you."

We knew about the mestizo tradition of embracing when people say hello or goodbye, but we never did that in our community. Of course, we knew what hugs were. When we were babies everyone hugged us. When we were growing up, we would hug each other, but it was more like a natural thing that children do, not a tradition we were supposed to follow. Of course husbands and wives hugged each other, but not in public.

When Madre Ester first hugged us it felt strange, but I became accustomed to it and started to enjoy her arms around me. Many years later when foreigners began coming to meet the Zapatistas in Chenalhó, we received many hugs. Embracing us was a way that the foreigners showed us "solidaridad," a castellano word I learned during that time. The word didn't teach me anything I didn't already know, but I liked how it tumbled off my tongue when I said it.

I didn't need the hugs either, but I got used to them.

A WHITE SWEATER

IT WAS FEBRUARY. Three months had passed since Verónica started working for Telling Our Stories. It was finally time to receive her first paycheck. She was excited to have some money. She had had to wait a long time to be paid. At a meeting in January, Diana apologized to her and the other girls because the money hadn't come in yet, and that's why they would have to wait a little longer to be paid.

At first I was worried. Even though Telling Our Stories isn't a government project, what was happening with my daughter's pay reminded me of what happened to me and the other women when we sold our weavings at the government handicraft store. We'd wait months to receive our money. Meanwhile we needed to buy things we couldn't raise or make.

But I told Verónica we would just have to wait and see if we could trust Diana. From what Verónica said, Diana wasn't like some of the mestizas we know who live in the lum. She treats Verónica and the other girls with respect.

Anyway my daughter was enjoying her work, and she was learning a lot.

On payday, we went together to San Cristóbal to pick up Verónica's check. Verónica went straight to the Telling Our Stories office, and I went to the co-op store to deliver some weavings to sell from my group in Lokan. We decided to meet at the bank after our errands. I arrived first and waited for Verónica. Finally I saw her running across the street to meet me. She had a big smile on her face.

"I got it, Mother! Diana was very nice to me. She asked me about how our work together has been going. Then she said she was looking forward to reading Lucia's story. She apologized for the delay in getting my check, and then she handed me a big white envelope with my paycheck! We can trust her, Mother!"

"That's good, daughter." I was happy for Verónica to have this money for all her hard work. I told her we better get in line at the bank. It wasn't that long. Soon we found ourselves with money stuffed inside our purses, and a day of shopping ahead of us. We tucked our purses in the folds of our wide belts. I carried half of Verónica's money because Victorio told us to divide her paycheck between us in case someone tried to rob us.

Ever since she started working for Telling Our Stories, Verónica had been dreaming about buying a new sweater. That's about all she had been talking about for the past week!

Whenever we went to the city to buy a sweater in the past, I had to make Verónica choose one from the piles of used clothes in the market. She would search for a pink or blue sweater, but she always had to settle for some other color. Often the sweater would be too big or stretched out and stained, or missing a button. I felt bad for my daughter that I couldn't afford to buy her a new one.

Finally, she had her own money to buy a brand new sweater—and other things too, if she wanted them.

The air was warming up when we came out of the bank, though the city always seems colder than Lokan. We blended into the crowds of women and men, kaxlan and indigenous, walking on the narrow stone sidewalks past shops full of all kinds of things. We stopped to look in the window with shoes of many colors and styles. I knew this store, but Verónica had never seen it. She bent over to look closely at a pair of red shoes with high heels. We've never worn anything but plastic sandals. But this store didn't sell cheap shoes, so we walked on.

I made a mental note to remind Verónica to buy a pair of sandals to replace her worn-out pair.

When we came to the plaza in front of the cathedral, we sat down by three tall crosses near two kaxlan women who seemed to be waiting for someone. After a while they waved at a woman walking toward them. Then the two got up and walked off arm and arm together with the woman. Verónica had been watching the women. "When you come to the city, do you ever wonder where all the people are going? Where do you think those women are going? Maybe to a restaurant or to work?

"You've come to San Cristóbal with me enough times to know that I'm usually too busy to look at people. I just go to the stores where I need to buy things and head home when I'm done."

But this day we weren't in a hurry. I got caught up with Verónica watching the people. I noticed the tourists making their way across the plaza, stopping to take photos of the cathedral.

One couple carried backpacks and wore puffy pants tied at their ankles. The pants were made of patches of the cloth that Guatemalan vendors sell in the market near the church of Santo Domingo. One of them wore his hair in dozens of long braids. It looked like he hadn't combed it in a long time. The couple stopped not far from me when three little girls from Chamula came running up to try to sell some woven bracelets to them. The girls held out long strings loaded with dozens of bracelets and when they reached the tourists they turned their faces upward, looked them in the eye, and said at the same time, "Buy one!" The couple stopped to look at the bracelets and bought one from each of the girls.

When the two reached the cathedral steps, another group of girls tried to sell them bracelets, but they didn't want to buy any more and told them "No, thank you." Actually, they told them "No, thank you" many times before the girls went away.

Soon the little girls found a new customer and ran after him, but he wouldn't stop. When the girls kept following him, he turned around and shooed them away, like bothersome dogs. It made me angry to see the little vendors treated this way, but I also thought about how it must feel to be a tourist trying to walk peacefully through the plaza while a little girl stops him every few feet, demanding he buy something.

The bells filled the plaza with a beautiful sound. They were announcing the next mass. I told Verónica that we should go inside and say a prayer of thanks for her job.

Verónica had only one thing on her mind—shopping—but she followed me inside. We entered through the huge wooden doors, crossed ourselves, and then found a place to kneel near the back. After we said our prayers and got back on our feet, I paused before leaving to let my eyes wander around the cathedral. Here and there were statues of saints and vases of lilies and other beautiful flowers. I took a deep breath and my whole body filled with the fragrance of flowers, incense, and candle smoke.

I looked up at the ceiling, covered with thousands of little wooden squares, and saw something I'd never seen before. Just below the ceiling two men dressed in white coats were standing on a platform with paint brushes in their hands. I whispered to my daughter, "Look at the men up there!" Verónica followed my finger to the two men walking along a narrow plank like sure-footed cats. We watched as they bent over paint cans and then got back up to stroke the white beams that held up the ceiling. Their movements looked like silent prayers to God.

I began to wonder if He comes close to them while they work. I asked my daughter if she thought that God talked to them. And if he did, what he would say.

"Oh, Mother. How could God talk to them?"

"I like to think He could," I said. "Maybe he tells them not to be afraid, that he will protect them while they paint. How do you think the painters might feel when they hear his voice? Maybe their feet become steadier. Maybe little wings sprout from their sides and push against the seams of their coats, ready to lift them up if they fall."

Verónica tugged on my arm and asked me, "What do you think happens to them when they finish their work each day? I bet you think they fly up to heaven to be with God! I think they climb back down and go home to eat supper."

My daughter was teasing me. I could have stayed all day watching the men paint and imagining what it feels like to be them, but Verónica was hungry, my neck was hurting, and we still had shopping to do. We crossed ourselves, genuflected, and walked out of the cathedral into the bright sun.

On our way to the market, we bought elotes covered in chile. I savored each juicy kernel. All the while, I couldn't get the painters in their white coats out of my mind. Then, to my surprise, Verónica said, "I think I'll buy a white sweater instead of a pink one." After yearning so long for a pink sweater, all of a sudden my daughter wanted a white one! Could the painters in their white coats have changed her mind?

But Verónica had trouble finding a white sweater at the market. She had almost given up and started looking for a pink one, when I saw some black and grey sweaters hanging on a rack in the back of a store. In the middle of all these old women sweaters was a white one.

I pulled the sweater off the rack. Had it been just waiting for Verónica? It gleamed in the light, especially around the neckline which was decorated with little roses in white and silver threads. I looked at the tag, and it wasn't that expensive. I held it up for Verónica to see and a big smile came over her face as she walked toward me. "I love it, Mother!" She held it over her chest. It looked very pretty against her black braids.

She paid for the sweater and put it on to go home. She stood out like a beacon of light as we made our way through the crowds in the market to a shoe store and then to a few stands to buy tomatoes and onions for our store.

When we got back to Lokan that afternoon, I had to catch up on my weaving. I was making Victorio a new tunic for Carnival. Each year I made him a new one to wear to the celebration in Polhó, the center of the Zapatista autonomous township in Chenalhó.

Although it had been a long day, I told Verónica that if she wanted to continue Lucia's story, I could talk while I wove. I didn't usually talk about Lucia while weaving because I have to concentrate on what I'm doing. But it doesn't take much concentration to weave a man's all-white tunic.

As Verónica went to collect her tape recorder, I thought about how good it is that we have a piece of clothing that's not complicated to make! At the same time, I wondered for the thousandth time why men's clothes in Chenalhó don't have any designs on them. In other townships, men have flowers on their tunics. But not the men in our township! The only thing they have to brighten them up are their hats with colored ribbons falling around the rim. While these thoughts were running through my mind, I realized that I hadn't told Verónica why Lucia didn't weave, only embroider. When she returned with the tape recorder I told her why.

WE WEAVE, WE PRAY

LUCIA DIDN'T KNOW how to weave because Carmela only taught her to embroider, but Lucia embroidered well. Her stitches were tight, and there were never stray threads hanging out of the designs. Sometimes people gave Lucia a little money when she prayed for them, and with that she bought cloth to make a skirt. She embroidered the seam of the skirt with flowers of many colors, and it looked very pretty. She earned money doing this for women who didn't like to embroider.

She had to buy her blouses from women who wove though. She never had more than two blouses because she didn't have much money. I got into the habit of giving Lucia my blouse when I was tired of it, because that gave me an excuse to weave myself a new one!

I remember that Lucia's shawl was a simple one made of white cotton cloth. On the border she embroidered symbols of Holy Cross. The rest of the shawl was almost bare, except for a few of our people's true designs that always look to me like the pawprint of a dog! I know your symbol book says that this design stands for the path of sun as it descends the veins of the ceiba tree. But it will always be a dog's pawprint to me.

Anyway, Lucia's shawl only had a few of these designs, and it was really quite sad.

Since Lucia didn't weave, she couldn't join the weaving group in Lokan that my mother and I formed soon after Hilario died. That was a big part of my life that Lucia and I didn't share. By the time Lucia was back to stay in Lokan, my weavings were good enough to sell to the tourists who came to visit San Cristóbal and at the government store there.

My mother was the representative of our local weavers' group. Her cargo was to gather all the weavings together that the members of our group brought to our house and take them to the government handicraft store in San Cristóbal. She had to make a list of how much she owed each woman. When the weavings had sold, she would collect the money and bring it back to the women. It's the same as today, except we don't sell at the government store anymore. Now we sell at stores that respect us and our work.

At the government store, the workers set the prices. Sometimes they didn't set them high enough so in the end we received very little for many weeks of work. We wondered if they were stealing the money they made from selling our weavings.

Whenever she would let me, I went with my mother to deliver weavings to the government store. That was most of the time, because my mother didn't speak much castellano, and the worker at the store only spoke a little tsotsil, so I would often have to explain what my mother was saying. Mother didn't like that I had to do that, but at least it wasn't as bad as when she had to go alone to sell to the tourist stores in San Cristóbal.

One time before the government store existed, my mother needed to sell a blouse because my little sister was very sick, and the doctor at the clinic said she needed medicine. I couldn't go with her to San Cristóbal because I had to stay with my sister. The owner of the store where my mother went to sell the blouse didn't speak bats'i k'op, and Mother only knew a little castellano. The señora took the blouse from my mother and held it in her hands for a long time, inspecting the work, as if she were looking for something wrong with it. Mother just stood behind the counter waiting patiently and trying not to feel insulted.

Finally, the owner said, "I'm sorry, but I have several blouses like this one that I haven't sold yet, and I have to sell them before I buy another. I can't give you money for this blouse, but I have a bag of apples I can trade for it."

My mother just stood there in shock. In one hand the woman was holding onto the blouse that had taken several weeks to weave, and in the other hand she was holding out a bag of apples. What was my mother to do? Take the blouse back or take the bag of apples in exchange?

It was late, and she would miss the bus to Lokan if she went to another store to try to sell the blouse. Plus, the doctor at the clinic had told my mother that my sister needed to eat fruit. So, with the doctor's words in her head, my mother took the bag of apples and left the store without saying a word to the señora.

After all her suffering, my mother didn't have any money to buy medicine for my sister or even to take the bus back to Lokan. So she started walking. If it weren't for the madres who picked her up on their way to Yabteclum, she would have had to walk in the dark through the mountains until the early hours of the morning before she arrived home.

My mother told me that day was one of the saddest of her life.

While I was busy weaving things to sell at the co-op store, Lucia was going to people's houses to pray. She was becoming well-respected in our community. The Believers wanted her to pray for them because she didn't use pox and knew the Catholic prayers as well as the traditional ones.

Hilario had told Lucia that it wasn't good to use pox when praying because she was still a young woman. He said that she should use sodas, which were becoming an acceptable substitute for pox among the Catholic and Protestant Believers.

Mol Miguel, who led Hilario's procession to the cemetery, always used pox in his healings. After Hilario died, he recommended Lucia to people who didn't drink pox and needed someone to pray for them. People told Lucia that Miguel had recommended her, and that gave her the idea to ask his help with something else.

Before he died, Hilario had begun to teach Lucia about plants to cure different sicknesses. Lucia knew a few things about plants from watching Hilario make teas for his patients, but she didn't always know which plants were used for which illnesses. She wanted Mol Miguel to show her where to find the plants, what their names were, and how to use them for cures. It was a big favor she was asking, so she came to his house early one morning with a bottle of pox. When Mol Miguel told her to come in, she went over to where he was seated and knelt in front of him and bowed her head. Then in the bik'it snuk', the high voice we used in the past to show respect to elders, she asked Miguel's pardon for coming to ask a favor. She told him that Hilario hadn't finished his work teaching her about plants and that she wanted Miguel to finish teaching her.

"Now, daughter, I need to tell you about the high voice in the past. It was very important, especially in joyol, when a boy's parents petition a girl he wants to marry. But we didn't use it only in joyol. No, we used it every day.

"I once had a cousin who knew how to use the high voice very well. Sadly, he died at a place near Comitan when he was still a young man. He needed money to petition for a bride, so he went to this place because they were looking for workers to build a road. When they brought his body back, they said that a machine had crushed him. I'm sure that if he had been able to do the joyol, he would have convinced the girl's parents to let her marry him, because he spoke in the high voice so beautifully.

"Once, not long before my own joyol, I went to buy something at my uncle's store, and as I was walking up the path to the store I thought I heard a strange and wonderful bird singing on a branch nearby. But then I looked inside the store and realized that the sound was my cousin Mateo talking to our uncle while he wrapped the candles that Mateo had just bought. Mateo's voice was high and sweet like a bird song. When I walked inside, Mateo was still talking, and my uncle had a big smile on his face as he handled the candles to Mateo. He was so happy that one of his nephews knew the bik'it snuk' well.

"When Mateo left, I tried to imitate his high voice, but I couldn't come close. I wanted to make my uncle smile, but the only thing I had to make him happy were a few pesos for some sugar.

"Now, let me finish telling you about how Lucia learned to use plants. It's getting late and we need to put the corn on the fire and get ready for bed."

Lucia's visit to Mol Miguel was successful. He agreed to teach her about herbs so she could not only be an j'ilol—one who sees—but also a j'ak'vomol—one who uses herbs to heal. From then on, Lucia was always collecting the leaves and flowers of plants. When I'd see her at the waterhole, we'd go off together and look for plants. Since not all the plants Lucia needed to heal grow in Lokan, we'd take advantage of our walks to the classes in Yabteclum to search for the plants along the way.

I learned a lot by accompanying Lucia. With what I learned, I was able to treat the many sicknesses you and your brothers had. Your father and I didn't need to bring an j'ilol to our house often, because I knew a lot about making teas with plants. Your father had become a prayer leader in the chapel in our community so he could pray for you too. When it was something more serious, we would ask Lucia to come to our house. When one of you was gravely ill or when Abolino's appendix almost burst, we took you to the clinic.

ABOUT LOVE

VERÓNICA AND I were sitting on the patio embroidering the seams of our new skirts when we talked about Lucia again. We covered our heads with our shawls because the sun was strong that day. The sun warmed my arms and legs and made the silver threads sparkle in the flowers I was embroidering. I had told Verónica that I would talk about Lucia while I was embroidering. Verónica asked me to talk about whether Lucia felt any conflict about being a healer and being a member of our religious group Word of God. I thought it best to start with the special course that Madre Ester invited us to attend outside of San Cristóbal.

The center where we gathered was outside the city at the base of a mountain. We thought about trying to visit Doña Dolores, but all our free time was spent with the madres and the other young women in the different buildings or on the patio and garden outside.

During the daytime, we sang hymns, read and discussed Bible verses, had coffee and cookie breaks, and ate delicious meals of rice with a chicken wing on top. At night we slept on beds stacked on top of each other. I remember the first night Lucia slept on top and after that we traded places. The room where we slept had a window with a view of the mountainside with densely-packed trees that seemed to go on forever. I felt a long way from home, but safe with Lucia and the madres and other young women.

In the afternoon of the first day, Madre Ester asked us to read a

Bible verse and act out what it meant without speaking. She said that since we spoke different languages, it could help us understand each other. She divided us into groups of five or six and told us to talk about how to present our Bible verse so the other participants could figure it out. At first everyone—even Lucia!—was embarrassed to do this. But little by little we liked how it helped us understand the Bible.

I remember some verses that our group received gave us a lot of trouble, but after we acted them out, we had one of the most interesting discussions that week. Our verses were from 1 Corinthians 13.

"Give me the Bible over there on the table, daughter. I want to read this very important part to you."

Verónica handed the Bible to me , open to 1 Corinthians 13:

"If I speak in the tongues of men and of angels, but have not love, I am only a resounding gong or a clanging cymbal. If I have the gift of prophecy and can fathom all mysteries and all knowledge, and if I have a faith that can move mountains, but have not love, I am nothing. If I give all I possess to the poor and surrender my body to the flames, but have not love, I gain nothing.

"Love is patient, love is kind. It does not envy, it does not boast, it is not proud. It is not rude, it is not self-seeking, it is not easily angered, it keeps no record of wrongs. Love does not delight in evil, but rejoices with the truth. It always protects, always trusts, always hopes, always perseveres.

"Love never fails. But where there are prophecies, they will cease; where there are tongues, they will be stilled; where there is knowledge, it will pass away."

Even though 1 Corinthians 13 had a simple message—love is above all things—it was very hard to show this! Marcela, one of the members of our group, finally came up with an idea. She said we could make a pyramid of our bodies. At the top would be love shown by two of us embracing each other. Under that would be Lucia praying to heal another member of our group. This showed how sacrificing for others isn't as important as loving them. Then at the bottom would be someone scolding another with their face full of anger and pointing their finger at the person to show how love does not get angry easily.

Because we couldn't actually stand on top of each other, Marcela and I asked permission to stand on a table hugging each other. Another group member lay down on a bench next to the table while Lucia prayed over her, and the last two members of our group knelt on the floor in anger. We hoped that this would show what the verse said, but no one figured it out. Except Madre Ester. She congratulated us and asked us to explain to the other members what we tried to show with our bodies. Marcela explained and then the other women clapped.

That evening Lucia and I sat on the patio between the buildings and talked with Madre Ester about love. Since we don't have a word for it in our language, we wanted to talk about how we thought about it in our hearts and how that was different from the way Jesus and the first Christians thought about it.

It was getting cold and Madre Ester buttoned her sweater up to the top, while Lucia and I pulled our shawls tightly around us. Then Madre Ester asked why we thought tsotsil doesn't have a separate word for "love."

We were quiet for a while thinking about the question. I didn't want to speak until I had a good idea of what my heart felt. I thought about how my heart is happy when I'm with my parents and Lucia and also how my parents are happy when they're talking with others in the Word of God meetings.

Then I said, "I think we don't have a word for love because it's how we live our lives. It's not something we need to say or explain. We look after each other every day. When we have problems we help each other. In Word of God meetings, my parents and the other adults listen a long time to each other, waiting until the person has finished speaking before they say anything. They don't raise their voices. They always go to the meetings and don't give up trying to solve problems, trying to make everyone's hearts equal.

"I think that's what love means, not giving up on each other, listening to each other, helping each other, respecting each other. We can't say I love you, but we can say kux ta ko'onton jme': my heart hurts for my mother. Or for someone else. When we love someone, we feel their pain."

Lucia looked at me with surprise. I don't think she knew that I had thought about love deeply. After I finished, Madre Ester told me that I had just described kanum bail, Christian love, a love that never ends, that just keeps growing as people accompany each other in their daily lives and struggle together for a better life, a life in which no one is oppressed or left out. I had never heard this word, but I was still learning many important words in our language and still am, for that matter.

Next Madre Ester asked us, "How do you say in tsotsil that a woman loves a man she wants to marry?"

Again, Lucia and I didn't have an answer ready. We thought for a while and then Lucia answered. She said, "You know that we aren't supposed to love someone who wants to marry us. We aren't even supposed to talk to them before the joyol! But when we're young and a girl's heart hurts for a boy or a boy's heart hurts for a girl, we say "scan smalal," she wants her husband. But that doesn't mean that their hearts hurt for the right reason. Sometimes they just want to have the person, like you would want a beautiful house. This kind of wanting love needs time to grow while two people live together and help each other, respect each other. In time, when one of them has a problem, the other one's heart hurts for them, and they would even die for them."

Madre Ester replied, "I think that's a beautiful understanding of love, even though I think that boys and girls need more freedom to talk to each other before they marry. Don't you?"

I spoke up again and said, "It isn't fair that I'm not supposed to talk to boys before one of them comes to ask to marry me. There's a boy I know from grammar school who I used to think about a lot. Last week on the trail, I saw him coming toward me. Since there was no one around, we stepped off the trail and went a little ways into the woods and talked for a while. After that, I decided that I don't like him that much, but talking to him made me sure that before I marry I need to hear how my future husband talks to me, if his words show respect for me, if they come from a big or a small heart. Then I'll know if I should marry."

When I finished, Lucia asked Madre Ester, "Before you became a nun, did you ever want to marry?'

Madre Ester took some time to answer, just as we had. These were hard questions. Lucia and I had never talked with anyone about the meaning of love between men and women. I don't think that Madre

Ester had talked much about it either. After all, she was supposed to think only of Christian love. Finally, she told us the story of a boy she loved before she became a nun. As she spoke, her eyes were on the mountains.

"I loved a boy once. We were going to marry when he finished university. Our plan was for me to finish university after we married, and he would support me working as a doctor. I was studying to be a linguist, a person who studies different languages. Guillermo was a very kind person and he loved me deeply. But something terrible happened his last semester of school. The bus he was taking to come home to Mexico City for Holy Week went off the road and crashed down the side of a cliff. Everyone was killed, except the driver who we later learned was drunk.

"I wanted the driver to suffer, even die, for what he had done to me and Guillermo. I blamed him for shattering our dreams. After the funeral I dropped out of university and spent most of my time in church praying or in my room crying. For a long time, I wouldn't see any of my friends because they reminded me of Guillermo. My heart was broken into many pieces, and I couldn't let go of Guillermo or my hatred for the driver. It was as if I had fallen into the chasm with my beloved, and I was just lying there beside his dead body suspended somewhere between life and death. This was my *noche oscura del alma*.

"I stayed in that condition for what seemed like an eternity. My parents were very worried about me, but they believed in me and knew that I would find my way back to myself. Then one day when I was in church praying, a nun came over and sat down next to me in the pew. Madre Carmen always greeted me when she was there, but she never did more than that.

"I heard the rustle of Madre Carmen's habit as she sat next to me, but I just kept praying. When I finished I sat silently beside her. Both our faces were uplifted toward the altar. Finally, Madre Carmen broke the silence and asked me, still looking at the altar, 'How are you, my child?'

"That simple question punctured a hole in the wall I had built around myself! Madre Carmen's words began to seep into me and spread throughout my body. I was still filled with loss, and I knew I wasn't well, but a feeling began to come over me that I could bear and carry my pain and loss, that I could go out into the world again and be a part of it. I couldn't answer Madre Carmen, but I think she saw something change in my face, and she took my hand in hers and said, 'Whatever is the source of your pain, you have the wisdom inside you to accept it and come out stronger when it passes. Embrace it, my child, but not in despair. Embrace it with joy, as your right to live fully all your days, no matter what losses you suffer along the way.'

"I don't know how Madre Carmen knew that these words were what I needed. I couldn't respond to her because I was weeping, but not tears of despair. They were tears of hope. I felt as if a light had gone on in my head where it had been dark before and now I could see how to live again, but not the life I had planned. I would have to live a life equal to the beautiful world that both Guillermo and I were born into, even though I would have to do it without him, and I didn't know what it would hold for me.

"I still felt pangs of loss in the months and years to come, but in those moments sitting in the pew with Madre Carmen I began to change.

"Not long after that day in the church, Madre Carmen invited me to volunteer in an afterschool program serving poor children who had migrated with their parents from indigenous pueblos to Mexico City. During those months of singing and playing with children and learning their languages, I began to live again and feel as if I had a place in the world and work to do. I can't tell you exactly when I knew that I wanted to join Madre Carmen's order, but I felt that God was calling me to serve Him. Eventually I believed with my whole heart that as a nun my unique self could finally be in the world in a way that made sense to me."

When Madre Ester finished, she turned to look at Lucia and me. Her eyes were moist with tears, but the expression on her face was full of peace, like those on the statues of the female saints in the church in Chenalhó. We didn't say anything for a while as Madre Ester's story entered our hearts. Finally Lucia asked Madre Ester, "What happened to your anger for the bus driver?"

"Oh, that took some time to pass. I think it began to leave when I started to care for the children. With them I was able to bring out the part inside of me that was full of love, not just for Guillermo, but for all my fellow humans. Finally, I realized that my anger toward the bus driver wasn't doing him or me any good. I began to pray for him, to ask God to forgive him and to help him stop drinking so that he'd never bring such terrible pain into the world again."

When Madre Ester finished her story, she rested her hands in her lap and looked first at Lucia and then at me. I wonder what she saw in my face. I had never heard a story from a distant place about people so different from myself, and I think it showed. Even so, I was surprised how much I could feel what Madre Ester had felt and how I understood the decisions that she had made. Maybe I could understand her because she spoke to us in tsotsil. I loved her for that, for communicating with us in our language.

Later, I asked Lucia what she thought about Madre Ester's story. She only said that she was sorry for her and glad that she had come to live in Chiapas.

Lucia and I had more talks with Madre Ester that week. A couple days before the course ended, Lucia began to question things that we had learned that week, such as what it says in the Old Testament about worshiping other gods in Exodus 23:13: "Pay attention to all that I have said to you, and make no mention of the names of other gods, nor let it be heard on your lips."

When one of the madres read this verse, Lucia leaned over and whispered to me, "What would my grandfather say about that?"

I shrugged my shoulders. Maybe this is something we don't have to worry about that much, is what I was thinking.

But of course we had to worry about it! It was one of the most important things in the Bible! I thought about my parents who believed in the Bible and still prayed to Earth and the ancestors. My father led prayer sessions in the chapel so it must be possible to believe in more than one God, or he wouldn't be permitted to lead the Christian prayers.

Later when we sat with Madre Ester during the break, we asked her about Exodus 23:13. Lucia opened up the topic with a speech to Madre Ester that I think she had been preparing since the course started. She spoke more loudly than usual. I could tell that she was nervous.

"My grandfather Hilario taught me that God is the same as Father Sun and that He, Mother Earth, and Mother Moon have equal power.

We pray to Earth to bring us good crops, we ask her forgiveness when we sin. We also pray to all the saints and they help us too.

"The Virgin Mary is the same as the Moon. She came to me three times in my dreams and gave me my cargo to heal. I pray to all our dieties and to Jesus and to Father God too. I can't believe in God if he wants me to give up praying to Mother Earth! We have to respect her, show our gratitude to her. She is our mother who gave birth to us and everything that exists. She gives us water to drink and to grow our corn and beans. She feeds us from her breast, and we pray to her and the angels that live in her that she will continue to give us enough to eat and that we won't suffer from sickness and sadness."

Madre Ester didn't look surprised by what Lucia said probably because she already knew a lot about our beliefs from living in Venustiano Carranza. But I think she was a little startled by the strength of Lucia's words.

We waited for Madre Ester to say something. Lucia fiddled with the ends of the fringe on her belt and pressed her lips together, moving them back and forth. Finally Madre Ester said, "I know that the ancestors are important to you, Lucia, that they teach you, that they come back to visit you on Day of the Dead and in dreams, that your dreams call you to do important things, like when Our Holy Mother came to you. You use the knowledge your grandfather and the ancestors gave you to heal people. You spread kanum bail to everyone you touch. I don't want you to forsake what gives your life meaning, to believe anything that your heart doesn't want to accept."

"Yes," said Lucia. "My religion is written in my heart, not in a book. I don't need the Bible to know what I believe. I'm sorry to tell you this because I know you want me to follow the word of God. You say things like God loves me, is with me, doesn't want me to be afraid. That's good. But we have powerful things in my culture that protect us too. Like moy. My grandfather taught me about wild tobacco, how you can blow it on the path when you're afraid and a flame or a light appears to protect us. I have seen this."

"I'm glad that your beliefs make you feel safe, Lucia. I just want you to know that God is also there on the path with the wild tobacco. He's whererever you are. He's like Mother Earth. He's calling all the people of the world to praise him in their languages, with their music, their prayers, with everything in their culture that is good. God's son is in the center of all the world's cultures, and from there he accompanies us. He doesn't tell us what to do or punish us. He only came to show us how to love one another. Can you believe that?"

"I'll try," Lucia said. She looked tired. It had been a long week, away from everything we were used to and with people we didn't know well. Madre Ester continued, "I have an idea I want you to consider. I'd like you to pray in the traditional way before we all leave to go back to our communities. And when we begin each course in Yabteclum, I want you to pray and also when we end. I know that it's an important tradition in your culture to pray before and after gatherings. I've been feeling bad that we've only prayed in the Christian way. We're fortunate to have a healer with us to pray for us so that nothing will come to harm us when we're together."

I was surprised to hear Madre Ester invite Lucia to pray, but Lucia seemed relieved that now she had a way to practice our traditions among the Believers. In a respectful and almost tender voice, she said, "I accept your invitation, and I want to thank you. We've never met a madre like you. Even if I can't take the word of God fully into my heart, I'll come to the courses and read the words from the Bible. I feel that I'm where I belong with you and Magdalena."

So, at the end of the last day, we gathered in the patio and formed a circle and held hands, all the madres and women and girls from different townships. Then Madre Ester said, "I've learned a lot this week from you. I hope you've learned a lot from each other and from the word of God.

"The other madres and I also learned more about your traditions. For example, in your communities it's important to ask an j'ilol to pray at the beginning and end of gatherings like this. We didn't think about that at the beginning of this retreat, but we can at least have a prayer to end our time together. I've asked Lucia who is an j'ilol in Lokan, Chenalhó to pray. Afterwards she'll give the words in Spanish for those of you who speak tseltal and tojolobal."

Lucia moved from the circle into the middle of the room. I followed her to set up the candles and light the incense. Then I slipped back into the circle while Lucia knelt and bowed her head before the incense and rows of candles. She looked like a dark lily on a long stem bending toward the earth. Everyone bowed their heads in silence while she prayed.

I thought we were done talking about Lucia for the day, but Verónica asked me if I would speak the actual words of Lucia's prayer into the tape recorder. "I'd really like to hear them," she said.

"I can't remember them. " I said. "Lucia prayed for at least ten minutes, and she used many words that only healers know. Anyway, I've talked enough for today."

I could tell that Verónica was disappointed that I didn't remember the prayer, but what could I do? I was tired of bringing back the past. So we stopped for the day. As often happened when we finished talking about Lucia, I got up abruptly and almost ran down the path to our store. I could hear my feet slapping on the stones. I guess I didn't want to lose any more customers. Or maybe I was relieved to be free of Verónica and her tape recorder.

I think I was feeling a little sad too.

WAITING FOR A BOY,
ASKING FOR A GIRL

THE NEXT TIME I agreed to talk about Lucia it was a rainy day—a Friday, I think. Victorio was at a meeting, all the chores were done, and I had time to talk. Verónica pulled two wood blocks close to the fire and set up her things on a little table nearby. By that time she was feeling comfortable using her tape recorder and didn't seem to worry about hitting a button by accident and erasing all my words.

At first, the possibility of her machine betraying us was always in the back of our minds. But when she replayed my words, there they were, just as clear as if I was speaking at that moment. I learned to enjoy hearing my words.

So before we began again, Verónica replayed a little bit of what I had said the last time we talked. We had finally come to the part in Lucia's story when she and I were at the age girls should marry. Over the years I had told Verónica how Victorio and I met and even a little about how he came to ask my parents to marry me. I'm glad that today some young men still do what Victorio did because it shows respect for the girl and her parents.

But Verónica doesn't think it's a good tradition because it gives all the right to the boy to pick a girl. Although the girl can reject him, it's embarrassing for everyone if she does. I went through that with the first boy who came to ask to marry me. Verónica had never heard the details about that bride petition, and she was eager for the chance to hear about it. I adjusted a few logs in the fire, sat back in my chair, and pulled my shawl across my chest as I always did when I started to talk. I think I was trying to protect what was inside my heart before I opened it to Verónica.

 I was seventeen years old when I met your father. It was in 1981 because we married in 1982 when I was eighteen. Victorio was hard working, and he was a prayer leader, like your grandfather. He was very respectful, never talked to me when we met on the trails. It helped that he was often bent over with a load of wood on his back and couldn't easily look me in the eye!

Victorio and I talked sometimes at the courses that the madres organized, but there were others around us so no one minded. I liked the way your father looked, even with the long scar on the side of his face. I liked that your father smiled a lot and how his eyes came alive when he read the scriptures. I said to myself, "This is a man I could be content with."

One day when we were waiting by the side of the road for a ride home from one of the courses, I asked your father how he got his scar. I wasn't usually so bold, but I wanted to know everything about him. When he heard my question, he quickly touched his scar as if he had forgotten about it. Then he told me how it happened, in a low voice so that others wouldn't hear.

"It was late at night, and I was walking home from a plantation where I'd been working. I was only a few miles from Lokan when all of a sudden a man came out of the bushes waving his machete. I never saw the man, only the machete which struck me across my face. The man must have been drunk and fled as soon as he saw what he'd done. When I got up from the ground, blood was streaming down my face and neck. I tore off part of my shirt to stop the blood. It was the middle of the night when I finally got home. My mother jumped out of bed when she saw my face and ran to find some pox. She quickly poured it on the wound and gave me a cup to drink. Then she took a needle and thread and sewed up my face. That's why the scar never healed too well."

Soon a truck came and we all climbed into the back. On the way home we didn't talk but I was thinking about Victorio the whole time and wondering when I would see him again.

It was only about a month later that your father came to my house with his parents to ask to marry me. A couple weeks before he came, my mother asked me, "What do you think about this boy Victorio? Do you want to marry him?"

I was embarrassed and didn't know what to say. Mother had never mentioned a boy to me in the same sentence with marriage. I told her that I liked him, and I thought I would marry him if he came to ask for me."

"Good then," my mother said. "We'll see what happens."

But then something happened that shattered my happiness for a while. I remember that day so well because it was the second worst day of my life up until then, the first one being the day my parents came to San Cristóbal to take me back to Lokan.

Dawn was still an hour away, and I was lying in bed listening to a high voice drifting over the mountainside. The boy was singing his petition as he came up the trail, and he was headed to my house! When he and his parents got as far as the níspero trees next to our house, the boy began to entreat my parents to wake up and let him and his parents into our house.

I heard my mother gasp and tell my father to get up. She realized that something had gone terribly wrong! Just the week before, Victorio's parents had invited my parents to drink sodas with them in the town center to prepare the way for Victorio to come on the first of the three visits he would make to ask my parents' permission to marry me. We were all happy. The first visit of the joyol was scheduled for a week later to give Victorio time to finish making or borrowing money to buy the gifts he would deliver to my parents.

We knew it couldn't be Victorio coming up the trail. Then who could it be? I peeked through the cracks in the wall. It was still dark, but I could see that it was Bernabe, the boy I knew from grammar school who I talked about when I complained to Madre Ester that girls aren't allowed to talk to boys before we marry. When I talked to Bernabe that day on the trail, I thought I made it clear that I wasn't interested in marrying him. Who was he to think that he could ignore my wishes? Why didn't his parents talk to mine first?

When things like this happened in the past, sometimes the girl and her family escaped from the house and hid in the woods until the boy and his parents left. But we didn't have time for that. My parents were sitting on the edge of their bed with their heads in their hands in a kind of frozen state. Then all of a sudden my mother bolted into action and told me to get up and help her make coffee for our guests.

"Daughter, comb your hair, put your best blouse on," she said.

"But I don't care how I look!" I told her. "I don't want to marry this boy! You've got to tell him that I don't want him. I'm waiting for Victorio."

"But what can we do? They're almost at the door? I have to invite them in."

"I've heard that Bernabe drinks beer in the town center with the bus drivers, and his parents aren't Believers. You don't want me to marry a drunk who will beat me and make my life miserable, do you?"

My mother gave me a look that said she knew that Bernabe would not be a good husband for me, but we didn't have time to talk. I left things in my parent's hands. As it turned out, they respected my wishes.

"So, what happened, Mother? How did you get out of marrying Bernabe?" Verónica asked.

"Do you really need to know this? What about the people who will read the book? Maybe Bernabe's children will read it and be upset that I talked about his failed joyol."

Verónica hadn't thought about what might happen if my words came out in a book. I think she thought that people of my generation in Chenalhó would never read the book. But now some of their children and grandchildren are going to high school and even university. Their teachers could have them read the book!

I didn't think that Bernabe's children or grandchildren would be offended if they read the part about their grandfather, but that gave Verónica an idea. She suggested that we use false names for the people who weren't that important in my story.

"Well, I don't know how these things are done, but if you think that will work, then I'll tell you the story of Bernabe's failed joyol. But then what will we do when I come to your uncle's petition to marry Lucia?"

"What!" Verónica exclaimed. I had never told her that my brother asked to marry Lucia. "I thought Lucia never wanted to marry and that young men didn't want to marry her because she was a healer and wouldn't be able to be a normal wife."

"Yes, that's true," I replied, "but Ricardo was different. He had always liked Lucia. Remember, he followed her failed attempt to go on in school and delivered her letter to Doña Dolores and brought Doña Dolores' letter back to her. Not long before he and my parents went to see Carmela, Lucia came to our house to pray for him.

"Ricardo had been trying to tie a load of wood on our horse's back, but something scared the animal and he reared up. All the wood came spilling off his back and onto Ricardo, and then the horse's hoofs came down on him too. When Ricardo finally returned that night, he could barely walk.

"The next day he couldn't get out of bed because his muscles wouldn't work. Lucia prayed a long time for Ricardo and gave him some salve from a special plant to put on his joints and all over his arms and legs. It didn't take long before the aches left his body, and he could sleep and work again. He fell in love with Lucia after that."

"Oh, dear God," Verónica said. "How can we handle all these problems of offending people?" Verónica was still taking in the news that Ricardo had wanted to marry Lucia. She was staring off into space, her face pinched together, like she was trying to figure out how the threads would come together in a new design.

I twirled the fringe on the edge of my shawl. I thought about how to help my daughter. Finally I came up with a solution.

"Daughter, I won't tell all the details of what happened with Bernabe, and when you write up my words, you can use a false name for him. As for your uncle, we can't use a false name for him, but we don't have to include the details of his joyol in Lucia's story. I will give a short version for the tape recorder. Then you'll turn it off, and I'll tell you the whole story."

I was starting to understand better than Verónica how to tell Lucia's story! Verónica thanked me for solving our problem and said, "Now please tell me the story of Ricardo's joyol! I can't wait to hear it."

"First, we have to finish with Bernabe," I said. "I'll just give a brief report, so turn the machine on, and we'll take care of that." Verónica turned the recorder on, and I continued.

When Bernabe and his parents were a few yards from the door, my father called for them to come into the house. I stood with my face to the wall and listened as Bernabe sat down beside my father, and Bernabe's parents knelt before my father and mother to begin their request on their son's behalf.

Bernabe's father knew how to use the high voice well. He told my father about the gifts that Bernabe had left outside the door to show their esteem for me and my parents and how their son was a good boy who would make a good husband for me.

Finally my father interrupted them and said, 'We're very sorry for your wasted effort, but our daughter's not ready to marry yet. She's waiting for another to come.' Bernabe's parents kept petitioning and didn't give up until finally my father interrupted them again. They paused and then Bernabe's father said that he could see that they should not have come, because, although their son was a respectful and hardworking boy, I wasn't ready to marry. Then they thanked my mother for the coffee and for listening to their request and got up. Bernabe got up too.

I had turned around by then and held my shawl over my mouth to hide my embarrassment for myself, Bernabe, and our parents. I didn't look at him. After he said goodbye to my parents, he went outside and put the case of soda on his back, the gift that he had hoped to give my parents to ensure that they would welcome him on the next visit.

But there wouldn't be another visit.

Although I was relieved, my heart ached for Bernabe and all the boys who go through great effort and expense to ask for a girl, only to be sent away.

"Now, turn off the tape recorder, daughter, and I'll tell you the sad story of Ricardo's request to marry Lucia."

Verónica obeyed me and turned all her attention to me as I repositioned myself in my chair and readied myself to continue.

Lucia and I talked often about my desire to marry and her wish to never marry. We both knew that no boy would come to ask to marry Lucia because he couldn't count on Lucia to be around all the time because of her cargo. Still, I felt sad for Lucia and wondered if she ever regretted that she would never have a companion, except her mother. When I asked her, she said, "No, I'm not sad at all not to marry. It's not my destiny. The only thing that worries me is what will happen to me when my mother is gone, and I'm old. Who will take care of me if I don't have any children?"

"My children will take care of you," I told her. "They'll be like your children, and you'll be my children's godmother, if you want to be."

"Of course, I do! Did I tell you that me' max has been teaching me about how to help women give birth? I've gone to a few births with her and I've already learned a lot. I can attend you when your babies are born."

"That would make me very happy," I said.

Between the time that Bernabe came to my house and Victorio came a week later, Ricardo got it into his head to petition Carmela to marry Lucia. My parents weren't unhappy about his choice. After all, Carmela was Ricardo's godmother, but his timing was very bad. My parents had just recovered from Bernabe's visit and were waiting for Victorio's joyol to begin. Without our knowing, Ricardo had used some of the money he made working in Cancún to buy gifts for the first visit of joyol.

I remember the day when Ricardo told my parents about his plans. He had just come in from the fields and was drinking matz with my father by the fire. He seemed nervous and moved a lot in his chair. Finally he said, "Mother, Father, I want you to help me go to my godmother's house to ask to marry her daughter. I've been thinking about this for a long time, and I've already bought the gifts."

My father was the first to respond, "But, son, haven't you thought about what it will be like to be married to one who heals? You won't be able to count on your wife to help you in the fields, and she won't always be home to make your matz or your tortillas."

"But that's not a problem for me. Before there were girls in our family, I helped mother make matz and tortillas. I helped around the house too. I haven't forgotten what the madres told us in the courses, that men should help women more with their work around the house and with the children. I heard them, and I'm ready to do it. You see, I've known Lucia my whole life. It's almost like she's my sister, but my feelings for her are more than that. I want her to be my wife and to share my life with me."

My mother then said to Ricardo, "If this is something your heart really wants, then we won't stand in your way. It would be a great help to Carmela if you were to marry Lucia. But couldn't you wait until after Victorio does the first visit of his joyol for your sister?"

My mother's request was reasonable, but when Ricardo got something in his head he couldn't get it out, and he was also very impatient. He was already twenty-three, past the age when most boys marry. After he dropped out of middle school, he helped my father in the fields, but he wanted to make some money so he left for Cancún to work as a bricklayer's assistant building hotels.

My parents didn't want him to leave, but the price of coffee was very low. They were worried about where they would find the money to buy the corn they couldn't grow, so they agreed to let him leave for six months.

While he was in Cancún, my brother saved his money instead of drinking it up with the other workers. When he came home, he had enough to help our family and also to buy some of the gifts for his joyol. He told my parents that he had been thinking about Lucia the whole time he was gone and had decided that, when he got home, he would ask them to help him petition to marry her.

If I was sad for Bernabe, I felt really sad for my brother because I knew Lucia would reject him, and I didn't know how he would react with his heart set on marrying her. He never asked me anything about Lucia even though he knew we were best friends. If he had, I could have told him that she didn't want to marry.

I wished it wasn't true, because I would have loved to have Lucia as my sister-in-law and to see Carmela and Lucia have the help they so badly needed. With his inheritance from my parents, Ricardo would have land for a milpa, and Lucia and her mother wouldn't have to work in other people's fields for their food. They would never be hungry again.

The day Ricardo announced his plans, I didn't tell your uncle anything. I was his little sister, and he didn't think I had any opinions worth listening to. Even though he was a good person to everyone else, with me he always had to show he was better and smarter.

But of course, I went right away to Lucia's house. When I arrived,

Lucia and her mother were just getting back from the water hole. I must have looked distressed because Carmela asked me if anything was wrong. I said everything was fine, but that I needed Lucia to come with me to check on my brother's bull that was tethered on land near their house. I walked behind Lucia on the trail and was grateful not to see her face as I told her about Ricardo.

"Something bad is going to happen, Lucia. My brother wants to marry you, and he's going to start the joyol soon."

Lucia stopped and whirled around. Her mouth and eyes fell open as if she'd just seen a ghost, like the day she came to school after her cargo dream.

"No, no, no! This can't be happening." Lucia kept repeating these words while we stood on the path. Then, just as suddenly as she stopped, she grabbed my hand and pulled me off the path to a grove of trees. She collapsed onto the ground and waited for me to sit down beside her. Then she tried to explain to me the real reason why she could never marry. I listened and heard Lucia tell me things about herself that I knew in my heart, but hadn't admitted to myself.

"I can't marry. I'm not like other women. You see, I'm not attracted to men. I don't have feelings for a man like you have for Victorio. My heart doesn't flutter when I'm near a man. When we were in school I didn't even have a crush on a boy! I've never wanted to think about how it would feel to be married, to sleep with a man. I don't know why this is so, but it's how I am. Ricardo is a good man, he's your brother, and he's my mother's godson, but I can't marry him—or any other man. I don't want to hurt Ricardo, but I can't marry him."

"Maybe you just haven't met the man who will make you happy," I said. I didn't really believe this, but I didn't know what else to say because I couldn't imagine life without a husband.

"No," said Lucia, more strongly this time, "I don't think there is a man in the world who could make me happy like that."

As Lucia's words sunk into me, I realized that I had never tried to picture Lucia married. She didn't seem to need anyone that much—not even me, her mother, or Hilario when he was alive. She walked on the mountain trails in the dark without fear. When she prayed, she communed with powerful spiritual beings. She didn't have to work her life around another person, except for her mother. She wasn't like any other girl I knew. Why should I be surprised that she didn't want to be a wife and mother?

But Lucia's words still troubled me because they meant she would never feel a man's warmth beside her at night. She would never have the soft bodies of her own babies and children to hold. We would continue to grow into womanhood differently and would not share the same feelings about many things. I had to accept that with each decision she made, Lucia was making herself increasingly more different from me and most women in Lokan.

After I talked to Lucia, I went and talked to Ricardo. I told my brother that Lucia would never marry, that no man could convince her to marry him. But he didn't believe me. He told me I didn't know what I was talking about. But then he changed his tone of voice and talked to me as he never had before or since, like a compañera, not a sister.

He said to me, "Little sister, you don't know what it's like in the cities. When I was in Cancún, I saw all kinds of beautiful women, from all over the world. Some had blonde hair and their lips were painted bright red. They were like strange and beautiful birds. At first, I looked at them a lot. I wondered how it would be to marry one of them. But they wouldn't even look at me. Or if they glanced my way, they would look straight through me. Indigenous men like me are invisible to them. Finally, I got tired of feeling that I didn't exist and stopped looking at them.

"Then my thoughts turned to the girls in Lokan, how beautiful they are in their traditional clothes and their long black hair. But when I thought about girls in Lokan, I kept thinking about Lucia. I thought about how she moves when she walks and how she looks when she's praying, how her hands feel when she's curing. She healed all of us in our family many times. Who knows if we'd still be alive if it weren't for her knowledge and power. She keeps the traditions, but she isn't afraid to defend what she wants and believes, even if it isn't what people understand, like when she ran away to San Cristóbal.

"I couldn't find a better wife in Lokan or anywhere else. I want to stay here and follow in father's footsteps. Life is too hard in the city. People don't have respect for anything, except money. I made money in

Cancún to help our family and to buy gifts to ask to marry Lucia, but that's all I was there for. You see, my heart has been yearning for Lucia for a long time, and I want her for my wife. I have to try to marry her, even if she rejects me. At least she'll know that there's a man who wants her and who will work hard for her and her mother."

After Ricardo finished, it was clear to me that nothing would change his mind and that no one could save him from the humiliation he was sure to feel when Lucia rejected him. I felt powerless to do anything to help my brother or Lucia.

I wasn't at Lucia's house for Ricardo's joyol, so I only know what Lucia and my parents told me and what I saw with my own eyes. Ricardo left for Cancún the morning after his failed petition. I'll never forget how he looked when he slung his backpack over his shoulder and thanked my mother for the toasted tortillas that she held out to him. He looked like he'd been in a fight, but it was just his broken heart that had burst to the surface leaving little red wounds all over his face. There were tears in both Ricardo's and my mother's eyes when he left. We didn't see him for a long time after that.

My parents were also deeply disturbed by what had happened at Carmela's house, but they were more exhausted than anything when they returned. I didn't ask them what had happened. I just waited until after Ricardo left to go see Lucia.

Fortunately, Lucia was home alone when I arrived, sitting by the fire with her arms folded around her. She looked like a kitten who had been attacked by a wild dog and was curled up by the fire licking her wounds.

Why do our traditions hurt people so much?

She pulled a wooden block over to the fire for me. I sat down beside her. "Ricardo left for Cancún today," I told her. "I just wanted you to know so you won't worry about seeing him on the path or anywhere else."

"So he left. May God forgive me for the shame I brought your brother and our families." Lucia covered her face and started to cry. I touched her knee to let her I know that I didn't blame her. Finally, she stopped crying and told me about the joyol.

"Everyone knows that I don't want to marry, but they thought I'd change my mind when I saw that Ricardo wanted to be my husband.

They didn't know how strongly I feel about not marrying. My mother begged me to accept your brother, but I told her I couldn't be a wife and a healer.

"It was so hard for her to tell your parents and Ricardo that I didn't want to marry him. When your parents were seated in our kitchen, my mother gathered up all her courage and explained to them that she didn't want to show them any disrespect, but that because I had a life-long cargo, I couldn't fulfill the duties of a wife, that it wouldn't be fair for me to make a man suffer by marrying me.

"Your parents protested, saying that Ricardo was an unusual man who followed the madres' instructions that men should help their wives around the house. They said that he cooked and cleaned before you were old enough to help your mother, and he made all his meals and washed his own clothes when he was working in Cancún. It would be no problem for him to do part of my work after they married. And he was ready to live with us for one year to help my mother and me. Then, after we were accustomed to being together, we would move to his land and build a house where my mother could come live with us so she wouldn't be alone.

"I was sitting in the corner of the kitchen hearing my life plotted out for me and feeling like I was going to throw up. I was terribly afraid that my mother didn't have the strength to keep rejecting your parents. But my mother told them two more times that she knew what a fine man her godson was, but that it wouldn't be fair to him to have a wife like me.

"Your parents paused before they spoke again, because they knew that in joyol the parents of the girl make her seem unworthy because they don't want to give her up. But your parents could see that my mother really meant what she said, that her words weren't according to tradition, but about something more serious. They looked at Ricardo who was sitting with his head bowed and holding his hat between his knees. I think he was trying not to cry.

"Your parents decided to end things there, and so they accepted my mother's words and apologized for bringing her any grief. Then they said goodbye and carried home all the corn, limes, oranges, bananas, and the case of soda that your brother had brought.

"After they were gone, I thanked God that nobody got angry with each other. I just hope that your parents won't blame my mother and me for Ricardo's unhappiness. I know that my mother is sad too, because she really wanted Ricardo to be her son-in-law, and I think your mother wanted me to be her daughter-in-law. Ricardo's almost like a son to my mother. If I had agreed to marry him, my mother's life would become much easier. She wouldn't have to work in other people's fields anymore. Perhaps God will punish me for being a terrible daughter."

After I finished recalling Ricardo's failed joyol, I picked up the blouse I was embroidering and Verónica filled a couple cups of water for us. Finally, Verónica asked me if I wanted to tell about Victorio's joyol. She was eager to record something more that day, since the full version of Ricardo's joyol wouldn't go into Lucia's story. But I told her, "No, I'm finished for now. Tomorrow I'll tell you about my marriage and how Lucia's life continued."

So Verónica picked up her tape recorder and wrapped it in the tortilla cloth where she'd been storing it. Then we went to wash our clothes on the rocks behind the house.

I DECIDE TO MARRY

EARLY THE NEXT MORNING when Verónica came into the kitchen, she told me she had dreamt about Ricardo. I smiled to think that my stories had entered her dreams. "Tell me your dream, daughter," I said. Verónica sat down and told me what happened in her dream.

"Ricardo was in Cancún working in a hotel where he met a woman like the women he told you about who don't talk to indigenous men. He was dressed in a white uniform that sparkled next to his brown face. His cheekbones arched up like wings, and he held himself tall. He was very handsome.

"The woman picked him out among the group of other young men waiting to help people with their bags and asked him to carry her bags to her room. They talked the whole way and once they got to her room they kept talking. She didn't want him to leave, but he did because, of course, he was working.

"Soon after, Ricardo asked the woman to marry him. She said yes, but there was a condition. If he wanted to marry her, he had to agree to live in the United States where she was from. He agreed, and they went to live in a place called Atlanta where they had a big house made of bricks, and Ricardo drove a taxi."

It might have been nice for Ricardo if he had married a rich woman from El Norte, but as it turned out he married a girl he met in Pantelhó when he went there to sell cabbages. Soon after he returned from Cancún, Ricardo asked my parents for some of his inheritance, and on that land he planted cabbages. He had heard that there was a big demand for cabbages in Pantelhó, so he took his harvest to the market there.

But when he got off the truck with all his costales, he saw that the market was filled with vendors selling cabbages. He didn't have any choice but to try to sell his crop, so he sat there all day in the hot sun trying to sell, but only a few people bought any of his cabbages.

Bad luck seemed to follow my brother wherever he went. But that day God must have wanted to make up for all of Ricardo's past suffering, because the girl who would become his wife came over to where he was sitting and bought cabbages from him. After she bought two cabbages in the morning, she came back later in the day to buy two more and this time she brought him a glass of atole from her mother's stand.

I think my brother fell in love with her because of that glass of atole. She must have looked like an angel to him, because he was hungry and thirsty and needed to save the little money he had made from selling cabbages to pay his passage back to Lokan.

It took a few months for Ricardo to make money to buy the gifts for joyol, but eventually that woman, Marcela, became my sister-in-law. Marcela's parents were happy to have Ricardo as their son-in-law, and my parents were relieved not to have to go through another rejection.

Now my brother and his wife live on land on the other side of Lokan, just beyond the Zapatista co-op store. In many ways my sister-in-law reminds me of how Lucia might be if she were here with us now. Marcela is intelligent and knows a lot about how to use plants to cure different sicknesses. When she comes to visit, I feel as if little bit of Lucia has come with her. I always laugh a lot when Marcela is in my house, like I used to do when Lucia visited.

I wanted to get this joyol business over so I could move on to another part of Lucia's story. So I told Verónica to get her tape recorder, and we could talk while we were making tortillas. Even though there would be a little slapping sound in the background, she could still make out my words. Verónica grabbed her shawl and looked for her tape recorder under a pile of thread on the table.

"Why are you in such a hurry, Mother?" Verónica asked me.

"We've talked too much about the problems of marrying," I replied.

"That's fine," she said. "But please don't rush through your joyol. I've waited all this time to hear how it sounds. You told me you'd give me the words so people will know our traditions."

"I won't rush. But let's get started so there's still time before I open the store to tell you about when Lucia helped me at your brother Abolino's birth."

As soon as I saw the red light, I began.

Now you know there are three visits in joyol. We've only talked about the first visit, because Bernabe and Ricardo never got past that one. If the girl's parents accept the gifts that the boy leaves on the first visit, then the boy and his parents, or whoever else he has asked to come and vouch for him, can return on a second visit. The families set the date for the second visit and the boy begins to gather together all the gifts he'll bring on the second and third visits, because he can be pretty sure that the girl and her parents will accept his petition to marry her.

At that point Verónica turned off the tape recorder because Victorio had come into the kitchen. She told him what we were doing. He chuckled as he pulled a chair close to the fire and said, "Your mother's parents really made me suffer!"

I laughed and said, "But you were so nervous, and you didn't want to live very long with my parents!"

"The two years of bride service that your parents wanted wasn't fair," Victorio said.

"That's true. But our parents finally settled on one year, and that was fair. And you know it wasn't that bad. My parents treated you like a son, and my father was always grateful to you that you encouraged him to plant coffee."

"Yes, it's true," Victorio said. "Working alongside your father in the fields was like working with my own father. He was also a good influence on me because he didn't drink like my father. When my year was up, it was hard to leave your parents, but we had to because it's our tradition."

"Father, did you have a ceremony when you and my mother left her parents' house to live in your parents' house?" Verónica asked.

"Yes, we followed the traditions. The day that ended my service, my parents came to my in-laws' house to ask if I could return to them. They brought one kilo of meat and a case of sodas instead of four bottles of pox, because your grandparents weren't drinkers.

"Then my father said, 'I came in order to talk with you because the time we agreed upon has come, the time when my son is to return to our house. This is why we came to talk with you and your wife, who is your companion, like your daughter is my son's companion.'

"As he spoke, my father got on his knees to ask pardon of your mother's parents because it was necessary to take their daughter from her house to another house. They drank the sodas, and then my father-in-law said, 'Yes, that's fine, we'll send your son and our daughter to you.'

"Before your mother and I left with my parents, my father-in-law said to your mother, 'Now the hour has come that you must go. But, daughter, remember that you always have your duties, your chores. Take care of your husband. Grind the corn well so that your husband doesn't suffer from hunger. Also, obey your father-in-law and mother-in-law with all your heart. Always ask your father-in-law if he wants matz or tortillas. Only in this way will you be content when you work together in the house and in the fields. It will go well for you in your in-laws' house, and you and your husband will become a true man and a true woman.'

"On all the major fiestas after that, your mother's father asked my parents to drink pinole and eat bread and meat at their house. When he saw my father-in-law in the market, my father would say, 'I invite you to my house to come eat because it's our custom, the way the ancestors did it.'

"When they finished eating, your mother's father would give my father a bottle of pox, because they knew he liked to drink. Your mother's parents would drink sodas, and then my father would say, 'Thank you for the food and pox.' Then they would talk about how your mother was adjusting to life in my house, and her father would tell my father and mother to come talk to him if she wasn't doing her chores or wasn't happy for some reason."

Verónica interrupted Victorio and asked, "Please tell me what your parents said when they came to ask Mother's parents if you could marry their daughter. Mother doesn't like to repeat the traditional prayers and petitions."

Victorio shifted in his chair, leaned over the tape recorder, and said, "I'm ready, daughter. Turn the machine on so you can hear how my parents spoke."

Verónica quickly turned on the tape recorder and Victorio began.

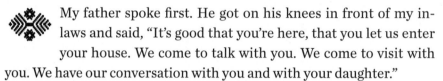My father spoke first. He got on his knees in front of my in-laws and said, "It's good that you're here, that you let us enter your house. We come to talk with you. We come to visit with you. We have our conversation with you and with your daughter."

"That's fine," my in-laws said.

"We come to visit with you and your daughter here in your house because our son, here, he fell in love with your daughter. Thanks to God and our Mother Moon, the Virgin of Guadalupe, that you have a daughter and that our son's eyes fell on her. We don't want there to be any lack of appreciation of your daughter or you. Let our talk be accepted. Let our children marry because it's our tradition, it's the way the ancestors did it."

My mother also said similar words, and then my father said, "That's fine, you see where we're going to leave these things."

We had left our gifts outside the door. "These things aren't for you to throw away, but to use. We want you to eat all that we've brought."

After your mother's parents accepted the case of soda, bread, and corn, we set the dates for the next three visits when I would come back carrying more gifts accompanied by my parents and my godparents.

I had to find the money to buy the gifts for all the visits, especially the last one, which is what mestizos call the wedding. I went to work for a few months cutting sugar on a plantation, and I borrowed a little money from my godfather. It took me a long time to pay him back because for the first year of marriage, I was only working for my father-in-law and not making any money.

On the last visit, my petitioners helped me carry three half-bushels of corn, a half-bushel of beans, a load of pitch pine, ten kilos of meat, bread, sugar, pineapples, limes, oranges, and three cases of sodas. We had to make a couple trips to bring all the gifts.

My mother also had to make pinole to drink with the bread. Before we ate, the elders gave your mother and me instructions about how to be a good wife and a good husband. Your mother's father read a part of the Bible, from Ephesians 5. The Bible is inside my bag. It won't take long to find the part. I've got it marked. Here it is:

"Husbands, love your wives, just as Christ loved the church and gave himself up for her to make her holy, cleansing her by the washing with water through the word, and to present her to himself as a radiant church, without stain or wrinkle or any other blemish, but holy and blameless. In this same way, husbands ought to love their wives as their own bodies. He who loves his wife loves himself. After all, no one ever hated their own body, but they feed and care for their body, just as Christ does the church—for we are members of his body. For this reason a man will leave his father and mother and be united to his wife, and the two will become one flesh."

When Victorio finished reading, he leaned back and stretched his arms over his head. He hadn't had any breakfast yet, so he went to find some masa and mixed his own matz. I put a plate of beans and a stack of tortilla on a little stool in front of him. It was silent in the kitchen while Victorio ate and Verónica toasted tortillas in the coals. I picked up my loom from the floor and put it around my waist. As I wove, I wondered what my daughter was thinking about everything she had just heard.

MY SONS ARE BORN

"IT WASN'T LONG before I realized I was pregnant. I was nineteen when I had your brother, Abolino."

Verónica had just asked me how I felt being a wife and living with Victorio. We were talking in our store, between customers. We had to take advantage of any opportunity to talk, because we could see that this experiment was going to take a lot longer than we had thought. Telling Our Stories expected Verónica to collect more than one woman's story!

"At first it was hard to be married," I told Verónica. "Your father and I slept in separate beds on opposite sides of the room for ten days. After that we slept together in the same bed with just a curtain between us and my parents and my little sister."

I quickly changed the subject to how happy my sister was when Victorio moved in. He joked with her and helped her behave better, which the rest of the family could never do. He also helped her with her homework at night. Even though he hadn't finished primary school, Victorio had learned how to speak and write Spanish well, better than me. My parents were impressed when they heard him reading from my sister's school books.

"What did Lucia say when she found out you were pregnant the first time?" Verónica asked.

"I didn't tell her right away. You know we don't tell many people when we are pregnant," I replied.

"But she was your best friend! Didn't you want her to know?"

"I wanted her to know. Yes, I wanted her to know. But we didn't see each other often after your father came to live with us. Things changed for us after I married. I have to tell you about that time, but first let me drink something. I'm so thirsty."

I went to the store refrigerator and took out a bottle of coke. I was in such a hurry to drink it that I used my teeth to take off the cap. Then I poured half of the bottle into a cup for myself and gave the bottle to Verónica. With my thirst quenched, I continued.

Lucia was busy in her cargo and also working in the fields with her mother. We would see each other at church on Sunday, but I didn't go to the courses in Yabteclum my first year of marriage, so I didn't see her there. But sometimes she would visit me on her way home from praying for a sick person.

The day I told her that I was pregnant was on one of those visits. The family at the house where she had prayed gave her a lot of dried beef, and she wanted to share it with your father and me. My heart was touched because her gift took me back to the days at school when Lucia used to bring me a piece of the beef she received at a healing with her grandfather.

We were alone because my sister was in school and everyone else had gone to pick coffee. I felt sick that morning so I stayed home to take care of things there. After she sat down Lucia asked me how I was, and I told her.

"I've never felt so sick. Each morning I throw up a lot, that's why I'm not in the cafetal with Victorio this morning. For a few months now I've known that I'm going to have a baby."

Lucia didn't seem surprised to hear that I was pregnant. She just said, "I know what you need for your stomach problems. I'll be right back."

Lucia went outside. In a little while, she came back with a handful of chamomile and jasmine leaves. She asked for some cinnamon and cloves, which luckily my mother had bought at the market the day before. Then Lucia made me a tea with these four ingredients."Here, drink this. You'll feel better."

I gratefully accepted the tea from Lucia and savored each sip as she told me about the courses in Yabteclum.

"The courses weren't too interesting for a few weeks because Madre Ester wasn't there. She had to go to Mexico City because her father died. She's been back about a couple weeks now, but she's still in mourning. Last week she looked tired and sad. Since I've been praying at the beginning and end of each course, I asked God to pray for Madre Ester's father.

"During the break, Madre Ester and I took our coffee and roll over to the tree where we used to sit with you. Right away Madre Ester thanked me for praying for her father. She said that my prayer eased the ache in her heart. She said that she was thinking of me when she was in Mexico City and bought me something in a bookstore there. It's a book about the spiritual beings that our ancestors worshipped long ago. She said it was only fair for me to be able to learn about my own people's history, not only the mestizos' history.

"When Madre Ester pulled the book out of her bag I couldn't say anything, not even thank you. I had never received a gift like this! Except for the food I receive at healings or what your mother brings us, the only gift I've received was a sweater on my graduation. Remember? Your godmother gave you one too. Just think of Madre Ester spending the little money she has to buy a book for me! Even Doña Dolores never gave me a book, although I think she would have if I had returned to work for her."

As Lucia talked, I thought about the gifts that I received from my mother-in-law when I married—a gourd, a tortilla cloth, and a net bag. These gifts symbolize my union with your father and will go in my grave with me when I'm buried—not the original ones, of course, but new ones to replace them. That thought made me wonder what Lucia would be buried with since she will never marry. Before I could think more about that, Lucia went on to tell me about her conversation with Madre Ester.

"Madre Ester asked me about my work as a healer, if I'm tired at times from having to leave my house at any time of the day or night to go to a person in need. I told her that I'm used to it, but that's not really true. At times I just want to sleep.

"It makes me happy that Madre Ester really cares about how I am. She asked about you too. I didn't know you were pregnant, but I told her that I was learning to be a midwife and that when your first child was born I'd be there to help you. She said to give you her greetings and that she hopes you come back to the courses."

I was glad to know that Madre Ester hadn't forgotten about me and realized how much I missed being with Lucia and her. I told Lucia I would go back soon. Victorio wanted me to go. But after I married things changed for me so that I didn't want to go far from home anymore. And then I started feeling sick every morning.

Verónica interrupted me to ask why I thought Madre Ester cared about Lucia enough to give her a book. I replied, "Maybe Madre Ester wanted Lucia to feel cared about since she didn't have a husband. It might also be because they had a lot in common being single women and spiritual leaders."

Verónica had another idea. "Maybe Madre Ester felt close to Lucia because she had confided in her about her boyfriend. I know if my friend had told me about something like that, I would feel close to them."

"Well, we'll never know what was in Madre Ester's heart, daughter. Now let me continue telling Lucia's story."

At the time, I didn't know that the more important question was why Lucia cared so much for Madre Ester. After Abolino was born and just before Lucia stopped going to the courses, my mother and I started going again. I saw how Lucia looked at Madre Ester when they were talking. It reminded me of how your father looked at me before we were married. I didn't think about it much at the time, but after Lucia stopped going to the courses I remembered.

But I'm getting ahead of myself. I haven't told you about what happened when Abolino was born.

"Don't worry, " Verónica said. "You don't have to go in any order. You can tell me more about Lucia and Madre Ester now if you want to."

"No, I don't want to. First, I need to tell you about how Lucia helped me at Abolino's birth."

"As you wish," she said, although I could tell she wanted to hear more about Madre Ester and Lucia.

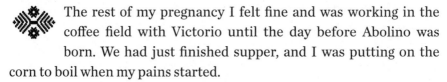 The rest of my pregnancy I felt fine and was working in the coffee field with Victorio until the day before Abolino was born. We had just finished supper, and I was putting on the corn to boil when my pains started.

At first I thought I had gas from eating too many beans, but then I felt a strong cramp around my waist. It stayed for a long time. I was so relieved when it went away. But after a while it came back, and this time I felt like corn must feel when it's crushed in the grinder. Later I felt like someone had their arms around me and was trying to see how tight they could squeeze me before I broke. The pain would leave for a while, but come back later, and I couldn't relieve it no matter what I did. I would get up and walk around, but it only got worse and so I would sit back down.

My mother told Victorio to try to keep me calm while she went to get Lucia. Lucia left her house immediately with my mother. Mother was running so fast down the path to our house that she lost her footing and fell, which she never does. She was panting when she finally reached my side. It seemed that Abolino couldn't wait to see his grandmother because after my mother returned, I felt him trying to come out of me.

Lucia took charge from then on. She pulled a chair close to me and instructed Victorio to sit on it. Then she directed me to kneel in front of him. Next, she lifted my arms and put my hands on Victorio's shoulders and told me that when the pains got bad to bear down on Victorio, and he would give his strength to me while I pushed the baby out.

Then she said, "I'm going to see if I can feel the baby's head." I had lost all my embarrassment and let Lucia put her hands under my skirt and feel for Abolino's head. "It's coming!" she announced.

At that moment I felt that my baby was pulling me inside to help him come out, and I got scared. Was I going to disappear or maybe die? Since I was the baby's mother, I had to help him, but I didn't have control of my body. "I'm coming! Open the door!" he seemed to be commanding me, and I felt that I had to obey him. So, I pushed with all my power. Then it was over, and I heard him cry.

My mother cleaned Abolino and put some salt on his tiny lips, like little leaves. "May you always have salt," she told him. She hoped he would always have money to buy salt and other necessities he couldn't grow, and also that his food—his life—would have some flavor.

I paused for a few minutes to drink some water. Verónica asked me if her grandmother had said the same thing when she was born.

"Yes, she did," I replied. "And I think God granted her wish because you have a job now and can buy the things you need. I think God has also been good to Abolino. He has a lot of coffee plants and can buy the things he needs, and he and his wife are happy together."

 Thank God my first son lived, because many children die at birth. Mothers die, too.

As you know, after I had Sebastian, I gave birth to another child who only lived two days. Lucia wasn't with me for that birth. She wasn't at home when Victorio arrived, so he went to find my sister-in-law Marcela who knew a little about helping women give birth.

The birth went well, but then two days later I woke up on the kitchen floor beside the fire on the narrow bed of boards that I slept on for several days after I gave birth. I felt content lying there by the fire with my baby sleeping in the curve of my arm. But when I tried to wake him, I couldn't. I shook his little body gently, but he didn't cry or move. Then I realized that he was cold to my touch.

I didn't want to believe what my heart knew. I moaned and called out to God, "Why did you take my child before he had a chance to live?" Your father woke up to the sound of my sobbing and came into the kitchen where he knelt beside me. After he realized that our son was dead, he started crying too. We stayed together mourning our son for what seemed like a long time.

But it couldn't have been, because soon your brothers woke up and came into the kitchen to drink their matz before going to school. Abolino and Sebastian were only seven and five at that time. When they saw us crying, they came up close to me and Abolino pulled back the blanket from the lower half of the baby's face. Then he said, "Mother, why isn't my little brother crying? What's wrong with him?"

I explained to my son that his brother couldn't stay with us, that he had gone to be with God in heaven. Abolino didn't really understand, but we left it like that and prepared to bury my son.

THE JAGUAR WOMAN

VERÓNICA AND I didn't talk again for a while. It was my turn at the Zapatista co-op store for a month. Each night when I got home from the co-op, I was too tired to talk. But one Sunday after church I said we could continue Lucia's story. This time Verónica was determined not to stop recording until I told her about Lucia's feelings for Madre Ester. But at the same time, she was trying to be respectful, to let me talk about what I wanted to. Which turned out to be my first year living with Victorio's parents, and then, finally, more about what Verónica really wanted to know.

Soon after Abolino was born, it was time to move to your father's land to live with his parents until we could build our own home, this house, the only one you've ever known. My mother and father-in-law weren't bad people, but I was sad when I lived with them because I missed my parents terribly. I wasn't like your father who liked living with my parents. I tried not to show my sadness, but it was always there in the bottom of my stomach reminding me of what I had left behind. My distraction was Abolino who could always make me laugh.

Two years later I had Sebastian. With the two boys life became busier for me but also happier. Your father and his parents were very content with little children in the house. Victorio helped me take care of them, and my mother-in-law often took care of the boys when I went to a course in Yabteclum with my mother.

The year that Sebastian turned one year old, your father and

I decided to baptize him at the Feast of St. Peter. I asked Lucia if she would be Sebastian's godmother, and she happily agreed. That meant that Sebastian wouldn't have a godfather, but I felt that Lucia was as good as two godparents in many ways. From that time on, Lucia and I were comadres, as well as friends.

But then things with Lucia started to change. What I have to tell you now will be hard for me to tell and maybe for you to hear.

I lowered my voice as if I was afraid that someone besides Verónica and the tape recorder would hear me. Verónica made motions with her hands to make me talk louder, but I didn't pay attention to her. I just moved closer to the machine and continued.

The year when Lucia and I turned twenty, I started to hear rumors about her that I didn't want to believe. Eventually I had to accept that some of them were true, like the ones about her getting drunk at healings. But one rumor I refused to believe, at least at first. It came from my aunt who told it to your father and me when we were walking home together from the market.

According to my aunt, one evening she was hurrying up the path to her house, trying to get home before nightfall, when she heard a cry that sounded like a big cat. But it couldn't be, because we don't see these creatures in our forest.

The cry got louder until my aunt saw what looked like a jaguar moving toward her a little ways up the mountain. He had spots and a long sleek body, and he made a whipping sound as he zig-zagged through the bushes. My aunt froze, believing that her life was soon to end.

But then, just as the jaguar was about to pounce, he rose from all fours to a standing position and his spots and claws became the clothes and hands of a woman. The jaguar-woman turned to look at my aunt, and then my aunt was truly frightened because she saw that it was Lucia! Before my aunt could call out to her, Lucia covered her face with her shawl and whirled around so that her back was to my aunt. Then Lucia lowered herself to the ground where she turned back into a jaguar and disappeared into the bushes.

At first I didn't believe my aunt's story, but later Lucia told me something that made me think it could be true.

I was alone making tamales early one morning when she came to visit. My mother-in-law had helped me wrap the corn and beans in leaves before she left to the market, and now the tamales were steaming in a big pot. Lucia was on her way home from praying for a sick person. I could smell pox on her breath when she sat beside me. This didn't surprise me because of the rumors I'd heard. But it still made me sad. I searched for a tamale that was cooked all the way through and put it on the table near Lucia.

"Eat, Comadre," I told her. "It'll give you strength."

Lucia accepted the tamale and started to peel off the leaf. I put water on the fire to make coffee, thinking it might sober her up. While I was looking for the coffee and sugar, Lucia told me something that Mol Miguel had told her the week before.

"Last week I went to see Mol Miguel because I had a terrible headache that wouldn't go away, no matter what medicine I took. It was the first time I had gone to Mol Miguel when I was sick, so he had never held my pulse to hear my blood, to find out what sickness I have.

"When he held my wrist in his hands, I saw a look of surprise come over his face, but then his look changed to one of a person who suddenly understands something they have suspected. Mol Miguel let go of my wrist and said to me, 'Your spirit companion is wounded, and he is a jaguar, the most powerful of all spirit companions. I remember now, that your grandfather once told me that when he pulsed you he thought that your nagual might be a jaguar. He was waiting to make sure. Your head aches now because your spirit companion is gravely ill, and this places you in danger. You could die. I will pray for you that your nagual heals quickly.'

"Mol Miguel prayed for me that day and the next. We went to a cave near his house for the last prayer. Inside the mouth of the cave, Mol Miguel placed candles and pine boughs and lit incense. Then he took a mouthful of pox and sprayed it all around the cave.

"While he prayed, he took breaks to drink more pox and spray it into the cave. Afterwards he told me that he did this to blind the Earth Lord's eyes so that my soul and my nagual could escape from the Earth Lord's prison. Mol Miguel prayed a long time to call my soul back. At the end of his prayer, he told me that my soul and my nagual were no longer in danger, and that my headaches would soon end."

Lucia looked me in the eyes and asked, "Comadre, you know what this means, don't you?"

"No, I don't. Did your headaches go away? What do you mean?" I asked.

"I mean that I've found out that my cargo demands more of me than I have to give. Only the most powerful healers have jaguars for spirit companions, but I'm just a young woman who learned a little about how to heal.

"Grandfather said that healers who have jaguars for spirit companions have power to heal like God—but unlike God, they can use their power to make people sick or even die. They can do the devil's work too. I have to control my spirit companion so that all his force goes toward good. I need to be strong to do this and look at me, I'm not strong!"

I looked at Lucia. Her calves and ankles were as thin as the sticks of my loom and her shoulder blades stuck out like handles above the yoke of her blouse. Next to her, with my round body and my ample breasts filled with milk, we had never looked so different.

Lucia went on to tell me that she was afraid of who she was and what she was becoming. "I know you can tell that I was drinking last night, but I have to confess, Comadre, I don't only drink when I heal. No! I take the pox home with me. After my mother goes to bed, I drink. I don't care about food anymore, just pox. This is who I am now. My grandfather would be ashamed of me. How can I go back to the little girl who the Moon Virgin chose and who grandfather showed how to heal?"

Lucia was crying now. I reached for her and stroked her hair as she laid her head on my shoulder. I looked for words of comfort and finally I said, "The little girl is still inside you. You just need to stop drinking to find her. The pox covers your eyes so all you can see is how miserable you are. Go back to sodas when you pray, Comadre. Your prayers were just as powerful when that's all you drank, maybe more powerful because you saw things clearly. After all, that's what a healer is, an j'ilol, someone who sees what the rest of us can't."

Victorio interrupted us with his noisy entrance into the kitchen. He laid his machete against the wall, put his hat on a hook, and plunked himself down on a chair. I got up to mix a little ball of masa in water as I've done a thousand times before. Victorio looked exhausted as he took the matz from me, but he seemed interested in taking his mind off his tiredness. So, he asked Verónica, "Daughter, tell me, how's your mother doing remembering our comadre's story?"

"Good!" she said. Verónica glanced at me. She was surprised, I think, that her father would ask her that.

"Has she gotten to the part where Lucia was drinking all the time?"

"How did you know?" Verónica asked. "That's exactly what we're talking about now."

"I can tell you something about that too," Victorio continued.

'Tell me, Father," Verónica said. She turned off the tape recorder and leaned closer to Victorio, waiting to hear what he had to add to my story. He took a couple drinks of matz and began.

"Before I married your mother, I was a drinker, like Lucia. You already know this. But maybe you don't know that there were rumors about my drinking too, about the fights I got into when I was drunk. I spent many nights in jail from my drinking. Then I had the dream I've told you about many times, when St. Peter asked me to help make balls of incense for the apostles. I took the dream to mean that he was giving me a cargo to serve him and all the saints.

"At first I didn't do anything about the dream, but I couldn't stop thinking about it. One Sunday in the market a catechist came up to me where I was drinking my uncle's chicha and asked me to come to church with him. I've always wondered how he knew I was ready to change, because to him I was just another drunk in the market.

"Inside the church I listened to the catechist read from the word of God, but his words didn't penetrate my heart because it was still flooded with chicha. The next Sunday when I was planning to drink again, the catechist found me before I started and asked me to go to church with him instead of joining my uncle at his chicha barrel. Maybe St. Peter was there with us this time, because I said yes and followed the catechist into the church. Listening to the word of God and talking with the catechist my heart filled with sadness over how far I had fallen from the young man who always helped his parents and was respectful to elders. That was the beginning of my climb back up from the low place I'd fallen. For Lucia, it was necessary to go to an even lower place before she stopped drinking."

IT'S NOT MY FAULT,
IT'S NOT MY CRIME

AFTER THAT SUNDAY when I told Verónica about Lucia's drinking, she had a hard time believing that the person I described was the Lucia she remembered.

"Mother, I can't believe that Lucia was ever the way you described. Lucia was always sober when I saw her, and she was always doing nice things for us and other people."

"Well, I'm not making it up, daughter. I would like to tell you a prettier story, but I'm telling the truth about Lucia. I know it must be hard to hear. You need to prepare yourself for hearing things that will make you feel sad."

I had to speak strongly with Verónica so she could prepare herself for the truth about Lucia. Verónica sighed and I continued.

After Lucia confessed to me about her drinking, I began to worry about her more and more. For one thing, she didn't want to go to the courses anymore in Yabteclum. When I asked her to go with me, she said they were a waste of her time and that she had learned all she needed to from the madres. It was sad to be at the courses without Lucia, but I kept going to them anyway since my mother always went.

Each time, Madre Ester asked me about Lucia. I didn't tell her the truth. I just said that Lucia was busy healing people and didn't have time to come to the courses. Madre Ester would always send me home with a greeting for Lucia.

I kept going to visit my comadre with food and greetings from Madre Ester but most times when I arrived she'd be at a sick person's house or in bed sleeping off a hangover. Little by little I stopped visiting her, but I never stopped thinking about her. Then one day my mother came by to tell me that Carmela had come to talk with her and my father about Lucia.

"My comadre says that Lucia is drinking all the time now. She doesn't work with her in neighbors' fields anymore. All she does when she's not healing is drink and sleep. Carmela wants you to go visit Lucia. She wants you to talk with her about what her drinking is doing to her."

I told my mother that I would go see Lucia the next day. She looked relieved and said she'd let Carmela know. I went in the morning the following day after I finished making tortillas, and my mother arrived to take Abolino home with her. Sebastian was still sleeping when I tucked him in my shawl and tied him to my back.

The rain that had come down hard the night before had left its mark—an arroyo on the way to Lucia's house had swollen to twice its usual size. I had to find a narrow spot to cross. A few years earlier a woman with her baby crossed that arroyo and was swept away and drowned.

The water where I crossed was shallow and, thanks to God, I didn't slip. Only my skirt got drenched, and Sebastian wouldn't stop wailing.

As I approached Lucia's house I could hear someone making tortillas in the kitchen.

"Are you there?" I asked.

"I'm here. Come in."

I stepped over the door frame. Carmela got up from her seat by the fire and put a wood block near the fire for me. I sat down and spread my skirt out over the fire to dry and gave Sebastian my breast. I'd been trying to soothe him ever since we crossed the arroyo. Even though he took my breast, he whimpered, and his little chest heaved up and down as he nursed.

I asked Carmela how she was feeling. She didn't look well. She told me she was fine, but Lucia wasn't.

"That's why I'm here. Mother told me that you'd come to see her about Lucia because she's not doing well," I said.

Carmela sighed. Then she resumed making tortillas and told me about how things were with Lucia. "Last night she came home from a healing very late. I was already asleep, but I woke up when I heard her enter the kitchen. I went back to sleep, but woke up again when I heard slurred singing coming from the kitchen. My daughter was singing, 'I'm a drunk woman, I'm a drunk girl.' But nobody was there to hear her, not even the arroyo was listening. You've never heard this song because not many women get drunk these days, except healers, like Lucia. Women sing it when they don't feel loved or appreciated. I don't know how to help Lucia. She seems to feel that there's no reason to keep living."

Verónica interrupted me and asked me to sing, "I'm a drunk woman, I'm a drunk girl." But I blurted back, "You always want me to remember embarrassing things!" She doesn't know how sad it is to sing this song and to hear a woman sing it. But then I relented. "Alright. I'll sing a little sample for you. But promise you won't laugh at me!"

"I won't, Mother! Lucia's suffering isn't funny. But her song will show how women use our traditions to express their feelings."

I lowered my head and began to rock back and forth in my chair, like I've seen my aunt do when she's drunk. As I rocked, I felt like a woman leaving behind everything around her to go deep inside herself. My voice became small and full of sorrow as I sang.

I'm a drunk woman,
I'm a drunk girl.
Yes, yes,
Yes, I'm a woman.

I don't have a father,
I'm a drunk woman,
I'm a drunk girl.
That's the way it is,
That's the way it is.

I'm going, girl,
I'm going, mother,
I'm really going, yes.

I'm on my way to worthlessness,
I'm on my way to death.
I'm a woman, yes,
I'm leaving, yes.

I'm a woman alone.
I'm a girl alone,
I'm a woman completely alone,
I'm a girl completely alone…

Lucia, woman I am,
Lucia, girl I am, so it is.
I'm not grieving in my heart,
because I will always be but a woman,
because I will always be but a girl.

Carry me away,
take me to a far away place,
so I may go, yes,
so I may leave, yes,
so I may get out of this, yes.

It's not my fault,
It's not my crime,
because I'm a woman alone,
because I'm a girl alone,

I'm going for good,
I'm going with the shit.
My head hurts, my heart hurts.
That's how I'm sick,
that's how I'm meeting death.

I'm a woman who has to die,
I'm a girl who has to die.

When I finished singing, I didn't look up at Verónica. I didn't know how
sad the song would make me feel.

"How are you feeling, Mother?" Verónica asked me.

I didn't feel well, but I told her I was fine. Then she turned off the tape recorder and said, "Let's go eat." When I didn't respond, she told me she was going to the kitchen. All the sad talk must have made her hungry. I imagined her ladling herself a bowl of sweet squash and corn and sitting down to eat, waiting for me to come.

As time passed and I didn't move, I hoped that she had put the corn on to boil for tortillas the next morning. Knowing Verónica, she was probably tidying up the kitchen. She liked things neat. She was a good daughter. Finally I heard her latch the kitchen door and go into the sleeping house. I should go to sleep too, I thought. But I still couldn't move. I don't know how long I dozed in my chair. Sometime in the night I finally made my way to the sleeping house and fell into a deep sleep.

The next morning when I entered the kitchen, Verónica was grinding the last of the corn to make masa. Before she could ask how I'd slept, I said, "Daughter, get your tape recorder, I want to finish talking about the part we started last night. Then I don't want to think about Lucia for a while."

"Thank you, Mother," she told me gratefully.

Verónica ran to get the tape recorder and sat down beside me while she set the comal on the fire to make tortillas. This morning my voice was normal, not sad and tired like the night before. Unlike a drunk woman, I wanted to be in control of my talk, even though my words were still sad. I started where I'd left off, sitting with Carmela in her kitchen talking about Lucia who was still in bed, hung over.

I told Lucia's mother that I would try to wake Lucia and talk some sense into her. Sebastian had fallen asleep while he nursed. I left him with Carmela and went to the sleeping house where I found Lucia lying in bed with her back to me. I came closer to the bed and asked her softly, "Comadre, are you awake?"

At first she didn't respond, but then she moaned and slowly turned her body towards me. I hadn't seen her for a few weeks. The change in her face startled me. It was bloated like a person who has been drinking steadily for many days. Her eyes were little slits on each side of her nose.

I moved my chair closer and felt as if I was drowning in a sea of pox. It was as if pox had replaced blood in Lucia's veins! How could this be my Lucia? I waited for her to open her eyes wider and say something to me. When she didn't I asked, "Comadre, are you thirsty? Do you want some water?"

Lucia nodded her head so I went outside to get some water. She needed help to drink, so I held the gourd to her parched lips while she drank small sips.

"Thank you," she said as she took her hands off the gourd and lay back down on the bed. We were quiet for a few minutes and then she turned her head toward me and said, "I'm so pitiful, even God doesn't love me."

I had never heard Lucia say anything like this before. I could tell that she had forgotten what we had learned in the word of God, that of all his sheep God loves most those who have lost their way. I had to remind her of this and so I said, "God loves you more than most. Every day you pray for others and cure them. It says in the holy book that when you do this for others, it's the same as doing it for Him. How could He not love you for that?"

Lucia looked at me with eyes filled with sorrow. She wasn't drunk anymore, just terribly sad. Then she told me what was making her feel this way.

"I didn't tell you the real reason why I stopped going to the courses: I love Madre Ester. I think my spirit companion has been captured and is being tortured somewhere, and that's why I have these feelings that I'm not supposed to have.

"When Madre Ester used to embrace us at the end of the workshops, I wanted to rest my head on her shoulder and not take it away. When I was near her I felt so happy, as if nothing could hurt me. I don't know the words to explain how I felt, how I still feel. I want to be with her always, like you must feel about Victorio.

"But women aren't supposed to love other women! When I became a healer, people understood why I had to be different from other women. But they could never understand this other way I'm different. I can't understand it myself."

I didn't know what to say to Lucia. What Lucia described feeling was the opposite of everything I had learned about women and men, so I needed time to think. But I wasn't surprised, like you might think.

I could see from her face that Verónica was shocked. It was harder for her to accept this new information about Lucia because she didn't grow up with her like I did. Verónica has heard about men who love men and women who love women, but it isn't something we see in our community, and the ancestors wouldn't have liked it.

Finally, Verónica asked me, "How did you feel about Lucia when she told you her feelings for Madre Ester?"

"I don't remember well. I think I didn't feel that Lucia's love for Madre Ester was wrong, even though others would think so if they knew about it. Perhaps I felt this way because I too had a lot of affection for Madre Ester. But I wasn't in love with her."

Verónica didn't say anything. I broke the silence and told her I wanted to continue, so I could finish with talking about this sad day.

I had to say something to my comadre to comfort her. We had been together since we were little girls. I knew her better than anyone. So I told her what was in my heart and hoped it would help her stop drinking and believe in herself again.

"Comadre, I don't judge you because I know your heart is big. It's very sad that you can't love Madre Ester the way you want to. But everything prevents it, her vows, our traditions. I'm sure that Madre Ester loves you as a sister, but she might not love you the way you love her. You've probably thought about this and that's why you're so sad that you're drinking all the time.

"But, Comadre, please don't despair. God doesn't give us all we desire, but He loves us and feels our suffering. You may not have a partner, but you have your mother and me and important work to do, and we need you to do it. Comadre, let's ask God, the Virgin Mary, and the mother-father-ancestor protectors to give you strength to stop drinking."

Lucia was sitting up in bed by that time. She nodded, smoothed her hair back, and got on her knees and prayed with me. After we finished praying, she took my hand and led me outside to the patio where the banana trees, wet from the rain, glistened in the sun. We stood in a patch of light.

Still holding my hand, Lucia said, "I don't want to feel sorry for myself anymore. I want to accept that I'll never have a companion like you have. I'm going to start using sodas in my prayers like I used to do. I'll try to stop drinking, but my heart needs time to change, and I don't know how much time it will take. In the meantime, I'll go back to church. I want to listen to the word of God with an open heart, but I can't go back to the courses again because it would hurt too much to see Madre Ester. When you see her, please tell her that I thank her for everything she did for me."

I told Lucia that I'd give her message to Madre Ester. I could hear Sebastian fussing in the kitchen, so I had to leave, but I told Lucia I'd be back soon. As I walked home, the trees and bushes on the trail were shining like they had just been freshly painted. I broke a little branch off a bush and gave it to Sebastian to keep him quiet. With my son laughing over my shoulder and the warm rays of the sun on my face, I thought to myself that God was telling me that Lucia would be all right.

THE SADDEST DAY

ALTHOUGH I FELT THAT GOD would make things better for Lucia, it didn't come true. Things only got worse. About a week after we prayed together, she must have decided that pox wasn't killing her fast enough, so she looked for something to kill herself more quickly.

We had just begun to talk about Lucia that morning. I was rarely sarcastic, and Verónica was surprised to hear me talk this way, especially about Lucia. She began to ask me why I was angry, but right then we heard Carmela coming down the path. I pulled a chair up to the fire for Carmela, and Verónica offered her a cup of rice atole.

Carmela sat down and watched as Verónica put her cup on the table beside the tape recorder. I had already told Carmela about "our experiment," so she wasn't surprised when she saw the machine. Then she asked how far we had come in telling Lucia's story. I looked down and paused before I answered. "Aunt, we've come to the saddest day in Lucia's life and yours."

Verónica didn't know that there was a saddest day in Carmela's life! Carmela must have seen the surprise on my daughter's face because she turned to her and said, "Before I lost Lucia ten years ago, I almost lost her another time."

I interrupted Carmela and said, "Aunt, would you do me the favor of telling this part of Lucia's story? Since I wasn't there, I only know what you told me."

As I expected, Carmela didn't want to be recorded, but she did agree to tell about her darkest day. Carmela set her atole on the table. I took up a blouse I was embroidering and kept my eyes on my stitches while Carmela talked.

After your mother came to visit Lucia, she didn't drink for about a week. My daughter wanted to change. We worked together in our neighbor's fields, and she finished embroidering a blouse that she hadn't touched for a long time. My heart was happy because Lucia was finally back to her old self.

But it didn't last. It didn't last. Late one night after she returned from praying for one of her god daughters, I heard her in the kitchen trying to light the fire. She was talking loudly to herself. Then she must have found a chair to sit down on because she began singing, "I'm a drunk woman."

I got up and told her to stop drinking and go to bed, but she just waved me away and said that she wanted to be alone. I didn't want to leave her, but I went back to bed. I kept waking up throughout the night, worried that she would fall in the fire and burn herself. Finally she came to bed, just before I got up.

For the next two weeks, Lucia drank every time she got a gift of pox. If she was paid for praying, she used the money to buy pox. I was afraid she'd kill herself from drinking, like some in our community. But mostly men die that way, not women.

One day I went to a course in Yabteclum with your mother and grandmother. I told Lucia that I'd be back that evening. She was still in bed hungover and barely mumbled goodbye. All day while the madres read from the Bible, I didn't learn anything because I was thinking about Lucia.

I talked with Madre Ester during the break, and she asked about Lucia. Something made me tell her the truth. Perhaps I wanted her to come see Lucia, which is exactly what she offered to do when she heard how bad things were. We made a plan for Madre Ester to visit the next day on her way back to San Cristóbal. Walking home, I was relieved knowing that Madre Ester was coming to see Lucia.

When I was close to home, our dog came running down the trail to meet me and jumped up on my chest, which he never did. He seemed desperate for me to follow him and even took my shawl in his mouth to make me go faster. I became afraid and ran up the path as fast as I could. While running, I saw a terrible vision of my daughter slipping away from me, flying up into the sky and disappearing into the clouds.

By the time I reached the kitchen door, I was panting from exhaustion and fear. I threw open the door and there was Lucia, lying on the floor beside the fire. A rope was tied around her neck and a piece of it was hanging from the rafter. I rushed past the chair where she had stood to tie herself to the rafter and took the noose from my daughter's neck. Then I shook her and called to her over and over, "Daughter! Daughter! Daughter!" I blew into her mouth as I've seen people do and kept blowing until I heard the most beautiful sound—a cough!

I drew back and saw her gasping for air. I held her while she coughed and coughed, trying to come back to life. Finally, I felt that she had come back because she wasn't coughing any more, and her eyes had opened.

Our dog got up from where he was lying beside us and wandered outside. He must have known that the danger had passed and soon I would shoo him outside.

We stayed there on the ground while my daughter rested in my arms. I thanked God that in her drunken state she had used a worn-out rope that wasn't strong enough to hold her weight, even though her body was mostly bones.

That night we were both relieved that Lucia hadn't been able to end her life. We didn't talk much. Just being alive and together seemed enough for us. But after we ate and before she went to bed, Lucia said, "Forgive me, Mother, for all I've done to you. I scared you to death when I tried to kill myself. I've made you suffer, and I haven't respected you. I want to stop drinking. And I will. I will. But if I slip sometimes, please believe me, I won't go back to the way I was, ever again."

When Carmela finished we sat quietly without speaking. Finally, she broke the silence and said she was going home. I watched her from the kitchen door, her figure becoming smaller and smaller as she walked up the path to her house. I felt sorry for having made her remember such a hard time in her life.

Before Verónica and I finished our work that day, she asked me, "Why did you talk in an angry way about Lucia this morning?"

I looked at the ground and spoke in a voice so low that I could barely hear myself. "I wasn't really angry. I was just remembering how I felt back then, that Lucia only thought of ending her own suffering, not about the suffering her death would bring her mother and me. I thought about how her mother would struggle on without her, about who would pray for all the sick people after she was gone, about where I would find another friend like her. I felt that Lucia didn't care anymore about God's will, about the candle in the sky that would go out in God's time, not in hers.

"But I forgave Lucia. Madre Ester helped me do this when she came to visit me the morning after Lucia tried to kill herself, which was also the last time that I saw Madre Ester."

DRINK THESE DROPS FROM THE
HANDS AND FEET OF GOD

LUCIA GOT UP EARLY the morning after the dark night of her soul, as Madre Ester called it. It was a good thing, because Madre Ester came to visit her very soon after. I learned about what had happened to Lucia when Madre Ester came to see me after she left Lucia's house that afternoon. We must have talked for a couple hours about Lucia. When I realized how late it had gotten, I was worried that Madre Ester wouldn't find a car back to San Cristóbal. So I walked her to the road, and we talked while we waited for a car. It took a long time for one to come, but of course when it did, it stopped. I envied the madres because when they needed a ride the cars always stopped for them.

When she arrived at Lucia's house, Madre Ester didn't know what had happened the night before. Lucia told her and then little by little everything, about her drinking, about her nagual, and about being different from other women. The only thing she left out were her feelings for Madre Ester, but Madre Ester seemed to know about them already.

She told Lucia, "I don't have to tell you that people in Lokan are afraid of anyone who is different. They think they can keep everyone the same by raising children to be exactly like they are. But when they do this, people suffer. You've suffered because you're different from most women. You must feel very lonely. I understand why you drank, but I'm so glad that you're going to stop, because with a clear head and heart you can keep going on, in a way that's true to you."

Lucia didn't say anything. I think she was still ashamed and unsure of what to say to Madre Ester. Madre Ester broke the silence and said, "Lucia, God loves everything about you and wants you to be free."

Finally Lucia said, "It means a lot to me that you came to see me. You've helped me a lot. I even learned something from the book you gave me about my nagual, and I'm not afraid of him as I was before. I would be lying if I said that I'm not lonely and sad. I think I'll always feel that way a little. But I'll never go as low as I was again. I'm climbing back up. I'm looking for a new order for my life."

Then Madre Ester told Lucia something that was a big surprise— she was being called to work in Guatemala. She would serve a pueblo like ours and learn another Mayan language. Lucia's heart probably sank into the pit of her stomach when she heard the news. I know mine did.

But she didn't go back to drinking. No. She was learning to accept loss as a part of life.

While we were waiting on the road, Madre Ester gave me an idea for how I could help Lucia come back to her old self. I have to give you a little background before I tell you her idea.

At that time, the Believers in Lokan were building a cooperative store. Madre Ester had heard about it and also about the threats from certain Believers who were no longer involved in the store.

The store was the first cooperative store in our township. We didn't go into it without a lot of thought. We wanted to offer a store for our community and to have the money stay in Lokan, rather than just go to mestizo shopkeepers in the lum.

The plan was for each member of the cooperative to take their turn at the store so we wouldn't have to pay anyone to run it. Our only expenses would be boards for the walls, tin for the roof, and cement for the floor. We thought it was only fair to our customers to have a cement floor. The men would build the house and the committee would buy the merchandise in San Cristóbal to sell in the store. One of us would be a treasurer to keep track of what we made and what we spent.

The Believers who felt threatened by us didn't really understand what we were doing and left when the work got too demanding. After that, they seemed to want us to fail because they started rumors that we were going to run all the stores out of Chenalhó. Another rumor said that we would only sell to fellow Believers, leaving the traditionalists, Presbyterians, Evangelicals, and Seventh Day Adventists without a store.

Madre Ester's idea was for Lucia to pray for our store, to protect it from envy. Of course, Lucia was the perfect person to pray for our store, because only a healer with the strongest nagual can defeat envy.

After I said goodbye to Madre Ester, I was sad to see her leave. I knew she wouldn't be back, but I also couldn't wait for your father to come home to tell him her idea. He immediately liked it and said, "Madre Ester is right. We need spiritual help to protect our store. But will Lucia agree and is she strong enough to pray against envy?"

"I think so, but only God knows," I told your father. "The store committee is coming to our house tonight. Let's ask them what they think of the idea."

Your father agreed. At the meeting that night I brought up the idea of Lucia praying for the store. A couple of our compañeros were not sure at first, but eventually they agreed because we were very worried about what might happen to our store from all the envy. Perhaps someone would burn the store down and all the merchandise before we could sell anything!

"Mother, wait. Before you go on, tell me about envy. I don't understand why it was such a strong force back in the time of the cooperative store."

Envy was not my favorite topic to talk about, but it was important for Verónica to understand it. So I told her, "Envy will be with us as long as the world exists. But in the time of the cooperative store, people thought illness was caused by demons in the earth—some that took the form of a snake—that could wrap around your soul and keep it a prisoner. People who wanted to harm someone—to make them sick or die—could go to caves and light incense and candles and implore the demons to take your soul and put it in prison. The sick person would need an j'ilol to go to the cave and light candles and incense to plead with the demons to let the person's soul go free. Then they could start to get well.

"In our case, we were worried that some of the members of the co-op who left would ask for a prayer to make one or all of us sick and or to make our store fail."

"But Mother, did you really believe that?"

"I did, I did. Who is to say what makes an insect that carries a sickness bite one person and not someone else? Envy explains what the doctors can't tell us."

Verónica doesn't believe what I believe about envy, but at least now she understands what it means. I keep trying to show her that we need the old ways as well as the new ones to make sense of all the bad and suffering in the world. I took a deep breath and went on to finish the story of the store prayer.

The next morning your father and I went to see Lucia. On the way to Lucia's house, your father spotted a honeycomb. He got excited and said that on the way home we should stop and get some honey. When I saw the honey I thought that maybe God put it there to remind us of the sweetness of life, and our comadre's return to it.

When we were close to Lucia's house, I called out, "Are you here?"

"I'm here. Come in!" Lucia said.

We entered the house and found Lucia sitting by the fire embroidering a blouse with saints, toads, and the true design in many different colors. This was the first time I had seen my comadre since she tried to kill herself. Seeing her whole and sober and creating something beautiful with her hands, I felt as if my old friend was back again.

When Lucia saw your father, her expression changed from one that told me she had some good gossip to tell me to a more serious one fit for the occasion. Lucia knew that Victorio wouldn't have come with me unless we had important business to take up with her. So, after we settled into our chairs, we didn't gossip as usual, but began our petition right away.

Your father wanted to show respect to Lucia because she was a healer and knew the traditions, so he got down on one knee in front of her and said, "We want to talk with you. We come to ask a favor. We have a cargo in the store, and we want you to help us pray for the store so that nothing bad will happen to us from those who envy us."

"Don't tell me that, Compadres! I've never prayed for a store or prayed a prayer against envy!" Lucia said with a little laugh. She was embarrassed with Victorio kneeling in front of her.

Then I said, "Let's drink the sodas we brought, your favorite apple flavor, and we'll see if our hearts can agree."

"Well, thanks, Compadres. It's nice that you brought me something," Lucia said.

Then your father got up and poured a little bit of the apple soda into a shot glass and said, "Comadre, drink these drops from the hands and feet of God!" Your father said this because by then sodas were becoming almost as powerful as pox in petitions and prayers.

Lucia said, "Well, I'm drinking."

After she returned the cup to your father, Lucia said what we had come hoping to hear. "I'll help you and the other compañeros because you have an important cargo, even if it isn't a traditional one. I'm honored that you believe in me having power to help the store."

"Thank you," we both said.

"Drink another little cup," your father said.

"Alright, give it to me, I'm going to drink it." Lucia drank her whole cup down, and then your father said, "Well, I've finished measuring out our soda. We only gave you a little. Forgive us our poverty, Comadre. We only came to see you for this need we have."

Then Lucia said, "Thank you, Compadres. Now we've drunk your sodas, the sweat from your labor. Take back your cup and bottle."

Your father took the cup and bottle from Lucia and put them in his net bag and then got up from his chair. Lucia and I stayed on our wood blocks by the fire.

"We'll see you tomorrow or the next day," your father said.

"That's good, we'll see each other soon," Lucia said.

"I'm going, Comadre," your father said.

"So go," she said back to him and gave him a big smile. Then she said, "May God go with you."

I stayed behind with Lucia so we could talk about everything that had happened since the night she almost died and the morning after when Madre Ester came to visit. We talked a long time. Lucia told me that she had stopped drinking and never wanted to go back to it. She was starting to feel that her life was a gift from God and that she needed to honor that gift, like Madre Ester had done after her fiancé died. Lucia said that even when she was lost in her drinking she sensed beauty around her and wanted to touch it, but it was always out of her reach. She felt that she didn't deserve it.

Lucia finished by telling me something that worried me at first, but then I understood what she meant. "All of my drinking and trying to kill myself was practice for how it will feel when I die. But when my mother rescued me, I never wanted to live so much. When I woke up in her arms and saw her face, it was more beautiful than anything I'd ever seen. Her touch felt like love itself. For a long time, I hadn't felt anything. When I was drinking the boundaries of my body felt as if they could fade into the trees, and I would cease to exist. But don't worry, Comadre, I'll never try to kill myself again. I want to live too much."

"Comadre, I'm so happy that you want to live. And I have to tell you that when Madre Ester stopped by my house to say goodbye, she talked about all the ways you helped her in her life and how much she learned from you. I think God gave you to each other for a while, even if it was painful not to be able to be with Madre Ester the way you wanted and to have to say goodbye. Lucky for us, we'll be here in Lokan forever and can always be friends."

As I walked home from Lucia's house I knew that she was going to be fine.

LET THEIR EYES BE BLINDED

VERÓNICA WAITED PATIENTLY for a few days to hear about Lucia's prayer while I took my turn in the Zapatista co-op store. But just as she was about to ask me to sit down with her, we had to leave the past and face what was happening in the present. Victorio was yelling for us to come help him! We ran outside and saw him above the house kneeling near his box of bees. Maybe they had stung him! People don't die from the sting, but it hurts a lot. I know because those bees have stung us all a few times. Once it took about a week for one of my bites to stop hurting.

As we ran up the hill I thought about how Victorio has always loved honey. He bought his bees to have honey and to make candles out of beeswax and sell them in our store. He learned to make boxes for the native bees that don't sting. But then the other bees, the African ones, had come into Lokan and were starting to fight our bees, and we were worried that they were winning.

When we reached the boxes of bees, some were still swarming above Victorio's head, but most had escaped and were flying up the mountainside. Victorio was kneeling on the ground beside his mule, choking back tears. The poor animal was covered in thousands of bites, and he wasn't moving.

I was wrong. Bee bites can kill, even a big animal. I felt so sorry for my husband. He depended on his mule to collect firewood and carry bananas and other things to market. Now he'd have to carry them on his back. "Oh, no!" I said. "I'm so sorry."

"No, it's worse. Not only the mule is dead. The bees killed our neighbor's pig too!"

Victorio turned his anguished face in the direction of our neighbors' patio. A wave of dread washed over me as I looked across the field. In my mind I could see little Ana Cristina, our neighbor's daughter, running home from school looking forward to seeing her pig and then finding him dead.

I remember when her parents bought the pig for her to take care of. For a couple years, she had been fattening it up and was planning to sell it soon to buy her school supplies. One day when I complimented her on her pig—she kept him very clean—she told me how much she loved him. She said she didn't want to sell him, because he had become like a companion, but she needed the money.

I sent Verónica to see the pig. When she returned she was crying and said, "He looks even worse than the mule. His whole body is covered with swollen bites. The poor creature's eyes and mouth are still open, and there are even bites in his mouth. How could God let this happen, Mother?"

I didn't have an answer for Verónica. I never did when these kinds of things happened. Finally we sat down beside Victorio who hadn't left the mule's side. I prayed a silent prayer for this poor creature who had suffered so greatly before he died.

Victorio had to wait until our neighbors returned from San Cristóbal to explain to them what had happened. He told them how their pig died and that he would pay them what the pig was worth. He offered to help them bury their pig and afterward the neighbor and his sons took pity on Victorio and helped him bury our mule. When Victorio got home that evening, he was the saddest I'd seen him since our little son died. I didn't have the heart to ask him about Ana Cristina.

We never found out how the bees escaped from the box. For about a week, Victorio stayed at home and didn't work in the fields or go to meetings. More than once that week when I went outside in the night to urinate, I saw light in the kitchen and Victorio kneeling before a row of candles. I paused and heard him praying in a low voice, like Lucia did when she prayed. I caught a few of his words and understood that he was asking God to protect us against envy.

Once, I felt a presence beside me and realized that Verónica had come outside too. She whispered, "What is father praying about?" She didn't want to believe my answer, to accept that people would envy us, but then I reminded her that her father is a Zapatista leader and that alone is enough to make people resent him.

For a couple days, we took a break from working on Lucia's story. We needed time to recover from the day of sadness. I finished weaving a blouse to sell at the co-op store while Verónica began a new one for herself.

She wanted to embroider hearts on the blouse. She had seen other girls put hearts in place of the true design around the yoke and wanted to try it herself. I liked how it looked and told her to keep going with it.

"Are you ready to hear about Lucia's prayer for the co-op store?"

It was late in the afternoon of the second day after our mule died. We were sitting in the kitchen where Verónica was working and all at once I stood up, put my hands on my hips and stood there, as if asking Verónica why she didn't have her tape recorder ready! I played with her sometimes, telling her I wanted to talk when she least expected it. She was surprised that I was ready to talk again, but a big smile came over her face, and she quickly laid her blouse on the back of the chair. It didn't take long before she returned with the recorder and notebook.

"Ready, Mother!" she announced. "Are you going to speak some of the prayer into the recorder? You know I want to hear Lucia's words."

"We'll see how I feel when we get there, " I said. "First I need to talk about how we got ready for the prayer."

The evening of the prayer—it was a summer night about twenty years ago—we met Lucia and the other Believers in the co-op store in Lokan. When your father and I arrived, most of our compañeros were already there standing beside a table organizing all the things we needed for the prayer.

Earlier we had taken a collection among the store committee members to buy the candles, sodas, and pox that Lucia requested for the prayer. The candles cost a lot! I think the big white ones were five hundred pesos at that time.

Edgar and Javier, two of the store committee members, had laid out, on the floor, all the candles that Lucia had asked for in three groups, for each of the three prayers that she would pray. She said she needed thirteen white candles for each prayer and some orange candles too, but I can't remember how many. Prayers to counteract envy always require orange candles.

Of course we also had incense, pox, and sodas. Lucia only used the pox to spray on the candles to blind the eyes of the evil ones.

Once we were together and had everything we needed for the prayers, we left for the lum where Lucia would pray twice, once in the Chapel of Holy Cross on the hill near the cemetery, and once in the main church in the center of town. We carried pitch pine torches to light the way because the store committee had set midnight as the time to start the first prayer. Lucia had told us that prayers against envy have to be done after midnight to make them work.

When we got to the lum about an hour later, we climbed straight up the hill to the Chapel of Holy Cross where Lucia prayed first. She knelt in front of the chapel with Edgar and Javier on either side of her, and together they prayed a few words, first to the crosses in front of the church and then to the closed door.

They said, "Through the sign of the Holy Cross, free us from our enemy, my Lord, our God. In the name of the Father, the Son, and the Holy Ghost."

Then Lucia opened the door and entered the chapel. We followed behind. The ancestors say that one can pray for both good and evil in the Chapel of Holy Cross. I don't know why Holy Cross allows someone to pray for bad things to happen, but that's what I've heard.

Anyway, Lucia needed to appeal to Holy Cross to use only its good power to counteract the envy we faced.

The church was cold inside, and it had very few decorations. I was glad that Lucia got down to business quickly so we could go to the church in town where there are many statues of the saints wearing beautiful woven blouses. I always feel closer to God there.

Once everyone was inside, Lucia directed Edgar and Javier where to place the candles on the floor. They started by placing thirteen white candles in the back row. Then in the middle row they put two bottles of

Pepsi on the ends and a Pepsi bottle of pox and a shot glass in the middle. In the front row the men placed orange and white candles, one white, one orange, then one white, then two orange, and on and on like that.

Edgar and Javier knelt on each side of Lucia and the rest of us knelt behind them. Lucia prayed for a minute and then directed Edgar to light the candles. He started with the white ones in the back. After the candles were lit, the three pounded their chests and bowed their faces on the floor all the while saying, "Through my fault, through my fault, through my fault." Then Lucia began her prayer. As was her custom, she rested the left side of her face on her hand and braced her left elbow with her right hand. I think it helped her keep kneeling for a long time.

"Now I'm going to read the words of Lucia's prayer. You didn't know that it's written down, did you?"

Verónica looked astonished. Then she said, "But why would Lucia write down her prayer?"

"She didn't write it. Another person did. A few weeks after she prayed for the store, someone came here, an anthropologist. I don't remember his name. He had learned our language and wanted to know about our prayers too. He had heard that Lucia knew how to pray, and he went to see her to talk with her. She agreed to say a sample prayer for him, and since the store prayer was still in her heart she prayed that. He recorded Lucia in his tape recorder, just like you're doing.

"About a month later, he returned with the prayer typed out on many pieces of paper and gave them to Lucia. Lucia didn't need it because it was in her heart, so she gave it to me to keep for the store committee, a piece of our store's history. Bring me the box under my bed. I'm sure the prayer is there."

Verónica didn't waste any time bringing the box to me.

"Here, Mother, do you know where the prayer is?"

"Yes, it's easy to find because I put it inside a piece of plastic to keep it safe."

When I found the pages of the prayer wrapped in plastic, I realized that it would take a long time to read. But I had promised Verónica to let her hear Lucia's words. I took a long drink of water and prepared myself. Then I began, using the same tone of voice and pace that Lucia used. My words floated away on the air as soon as they left my mouth. When one group of words left, another followed quickly behind.

"Merciful God, Jesus Christ, Lord,
Flowery Father, Father Holy Cross, Holy Virgin María,
I take this opportunity to enter beneath your feet,
I take this opportunity to enter beneath your hands,
along with your children, Lord,
whom you brought to light, whom you begot.

"Although my words aren't much, Lord,
nothing more than a word or two,
I am here with your children,
whom you brought to light,
whom you begot,
before your flowery body,
before your flowery face,
merciful Holy Jesus Christ,
Father, Son, Holy Spirit, Father God.

"That's why, Lord, it's been a while,
it's been a good while,
that some of your other children
have another way of talking,
have another way of thinking,
those that are gathered together to do bad.

"That's why, now, Lord,
the envy, the quarreling,
and also the anger in their hearts,
don't let it be fulfilled, Lord,
the pleas of the bad ones,
the rage in their hearts,
don't let it be fulfilled, Lord.
before your flowery face, Lord.

"That's why we've come on our knees,
and with our face to the soil.

We have brought our candles and our flowers,
that there be a change for our well-being, Lord,
for the well-being of our flesh,
for the well-being of our bodies, Lord,
Saint Jose, the Holy Virgin María
who is in the Center of the Holy Sky,
before her flowery body,
before her flowery face.

"That's why, please intervene, Lord,
throw the bad words to the side,
let all the bad words be discarded,
all the problems,
all the envy and sadness,
let it be erased now,
from your presence,
from before your flowery body,
from before your flowery face.

"The envy can't continue, Lord,
before your flowery face,
your flowery countenance, Lord,
Holy Sindico, Holy Jesus Christ.
That's why, Lord, we ask that
everything be the opposite of what it is.

"Let them go far away, Lord,
your children that you gave birth to,
that you begot, that you raised,
who want to do bad.
Don't let their hearts be like this forever,
always bad, always with anger,
with envy in their minds,
and in their hearts.
They always say about us,
'We'll see if they make a lot of money.'

"Please Lord, stand up and send your power.

Don't let them be provoked to do bad,
don't let them be deceived,
don't let them be idiots in their hearts,
or be distracted by something bad, Lord.
Don't let the wickedness in their mouths find a place to go.
Let their bad words be frozen in the wind,
let the wind take their words far away.

"Make the wind and the clouds walk on other paths,
that they don't find your children that you gave birth to,
that you begot,
that are here before your flowery face,
before your flowery countenance,
Flowery God, merciful Lord.

"Let them have their things, Lord, because for them
it's not possible to live without their earnings.
And also they can't work for the mestizos any longer,
because that way they can't buy the things they need.
They can't obtain the money to buy their corn,
the money to buy their clothes,
the money to buy their salt.

"All the wickedness that brings death, Lord,
don't let it be placed on their path,
don't let them step on the wickedness.
Don't let anything bad happen to them,
don't let them fall ill, or death come to them, Lord.

"Before your flowery Earth, please Lord,
fill the Earth with holy light,
let it always be clean,
before your flowery face,
before your flowery countenance, Lord.

"Holy Merciful Jesus Christ, Lord,
and all the holy beings,
let their eyes be blinded,
let their faces be blinded,

the bad ones, so they can't see what's happening,
and also blind the eyes of the Demon who drives evil.

"Please, Lord, cover their mouths,
and cover their lips,
so they can't go through
with what they are thinking about,
those who have envy and anger,
in their minds and in their hearts.
Don't let the words from their lips have more power,
Tell them the truth and show them clearly that they can't do
what they're doing, Lord.

"That's why we bring candles so you have more power,
in your body, in your flesh, Lord, Holy Flowery God.
Holy Flowery Jesus Christ, Father Apostle, Father Holy Cross,
Father Saint Jose, and Holy Virgin María.
Now, I ask that you unite
together with the owner of the skies,
together with the owner of the Earth,
together with the owner of the Holy Hills,
together with the owner of the Holy Mountain Peaks,
stand up and send your power,
stand together with the Sky and the Earth,
do me the favor of coming now.

"That's why they have come here enduring hunger,
these children that you brought to light, that you begot.
They are passing to you their flower,
they are passing to you their candles.

"Holy Mother María, who is in the Holy Sky,
bless my humble words,
and also my stories and my histories.
Get up and send your power,
stand up and send your power
over your children,

and all who are gathered here,
beneath your feet, and beneath your hands.

"Forgive us, from the littliest one to the biggest one,
flowery God, flowery Jesus Christ.
Let them never suffer strange dreams,
or some sadness in their hearts.
That's why I'm asking with my whole heart
for their well-being, because you are Lord.

"Now, Lord, I come bowing my body,
which has to end, which will decay.
I have to die, Holy Merciful Jesus Christ, Lord.
Forgive my flesh, my body,
that which is here seated beneath your feet,
and beneath your hands, Holy God,
that which is here kneeling under your hands
and under your feet,
so I can come closer to thee.

"May you accept the foul odor of my body before you,
and also that of your children whom you gave to light,
to your children whom you begot,
who are here gathered before your holy presence,
beneath your feet and beneath your hands,
Holy Flowery God, Flowery Holy Ladino.

"Father who is in the sky,
please stand up and send your power,
together with the Holy Sky and Holy Earth,
Holy Jesus Christ, Holy Sindico, Holy Virgin Mary,
and also, you owners of the Holy Hills
and owners of the Holy Earth
and owners of the Holy Mountain Peaks.

"Receive from me all that I bring,
beneath your feet, beneath your hands, Lord.
Merciful Holy Judge, Holy Virgin María

who is in the Holy Sky,
stand up and send your power.

"This is all that I want to say.
Forgive me as far as I could ask you a favor,
as far as I could worship you."

I felt very tired after I finished reading Lucia's prayer, but the prayer seemed to give Verónica energy, and she wanted to talk about it.

"Mother, listening to you read Lucia's prayer was like you were praying for real, as if Lucia's words still have power. You know I've never thought much about traditional prayers until you started to talk about Lucia. I have so many questions. But first, tell me, why would Lucia ask God to forgive the foul odor of her body and the co-op store members' bodies? What's so wrong with our bodies?"

I was surprised by Verónica's question. She didn't seem to have some basic information that I thought she had learned. That's what happens when we follow different ways, and we don't always learn everything we need to know about each of them.

"Because we humans are not pure, like God or Mother Earth. Our bodies smell. We spill blood, urine, and feces on Mother Earth. We ask God to forgive us our humanness. We might not need to, but we do it anyway. Now, let me finish telling you what Lucia did after her first prayer and at the next two prayers."

After Lucia finished praying, she took the bottle of pox and sprinkled it over the floor in front of the candles. Of course, she didn't drink any of the pox because she had stopped, and the Believers don't drink. She gave the sodas to Edgar and Javier who began to measure out cups for everyone present. They served your father and me first because we were the ones who had asked Lucia to pray. Before we left the chapel, she prayed a few more words.

When we got up to leave, Ceiba, one of our compañeros' daughters, was giggling because her father was asleep on his knees. Javier nudged him to get up, and we all laughed as he opened his eyes and realized what had happened.

We made our way carefully down the trail from the chapel to the church in the center of the lum. We only had a couple pitch pine torches to light our way, but no one fell and soon we arrived at the church.

It was about 4 a.m when Lucia started her second prayer inside the church. I don't need to give it to you because it was like the one I just prayed. The only difference between the first and second prayers was that Lucia didn't use pox in the church because the padre didn't allow it inside.

Too bad he didn't ban it inside the rectory! He was quite a drinker, the padre.

Even if he didn't understand why we were against pox, the madres did, and they supported us in our campaign to help people stop drinking.

By the time we had returned to the co-op store in Lokan for the final and third prayer, everyone was really tired, even Lucia. But you would never know it. She prayed with her whole heart for at least another hour.

When she was done, she announced "I'm finished," but only a few people heard her because almost everyone was asleep, sprawled out on petates and pieces of plastic covering the cold cement. Only Edgar, Javier, and your father and I heard. Your father and I had taken turns dozing off while Lucia prayed. We made the effort to stay awake because it had been our idea to ask her to pray, and we wanted to support her as much as we could.

Edgar and Javier were in charge of getting breakfast for Lucia. When they thought her prayer was almost over, they went to their homes to collect the breakfast for Lucia that their wives had made. We didn't want Lucia to wait too long to eat because she had really sacrificed for us. Seeing her slumped over in a chair trying to keep from falling asleep, I thanked God for helping Lucia find the strength to make it through the night so our little group could struggle for a better life.

Our compañeros came back with a special breakfast for Lucia—fried eggs in chicken broth, shrimp, refried beans, and tortillas. While Lucia ate, she said that she could do more prayers if necessary in a cave near Lokan, the one where Mol Miguel had prayed for her and where it was said that Earth gave the ancestors the first corn and beans.

We thanked her for the offer, but most of us thought that it wouldn't be necessary. And it turned out that it wasn't. After Lucia prayed, the people who opposed us stopped spreading rumors about the store. Little by little their envy and anger got carried away by the wind, just as Lucia prayed it would.

THE MOON VIRGIN COMES AGAIN

FIVE MONTHS HAD PASSED since I started to tell Lucia's story. Verónica's tape recorder had thousands, maybe millions of words on it. Words that I had given her. Some were even holy, like the words of Lucia's prayers. Each time we sat down together, Verónica seemed more interested in our work. She even showed me a different kind of respect, not the kind people receive just because they're your parents, but the kind that people earn by how they act and treat other people. We still joked with each other, and sometimes I had to correct misunderstandings, but I felt something growing between us that hadn't existed before.

Even so, sometimes I didn't feel I deserved my daughter's respect in the way she was showing it to me. One day, I was feeling unsure about what I was doing telling Lucia's story into a tape recorder. Perhaps that was why I touched the buttons on the machine, something I'd never done before.

Verónica had her back to me and was surprised when she heard a clicking sound. She turned around right away. When she saw my hand on the tape recorder, she yelled, "Don't touch anything! That's my job!" I pulled my hand back quickly, like a child caught in the act of doing something forbidden. I reached for a blouse on the back of my chair and soon the needle and thread were in my hands, and I was embroidering.

"I'm sorry, Mother," she said. "I shouldn't have spoken to you that way. I was just afraid you would erase your words, all our hard work."

I laid the blouse in my lap and sat still, not saying anything.

"What's the matter? Can't you forgive me?" she asked me.

When I finally spoke, my words came from the bottom of a deep well. My faint voice and the way I twisted my face as I spoke must have made Verónica feel that she needed to listen to me with her whole heart because I never saw her pay so much attention to me.

"I'm just a woman of the mountains, a woman of the hills. Even after all the changes that came to Lokan, I still don't know anything. All I know how to do is weave and take care of the house. If the madres and the Zapatistas hadn't come to Lokan, I would never have known how ignorant I am.

"Doing this project, I see all the things you know how to do, and I feel my ignorance even more. How I wanted to go to school when I was young! Why did I give up without a fight? Then after you met Rodrigo, I did the same thing to you that my mother did to me. I didn't let you stay in school. I made you choose between school and Rodrigo.

"Now, here you are living with us without a husband, when the other girls your age are married and having babies. For months I've been talking to you about Lucia, who tried so hard to be different, to be free to be herself, but all the time I'm thinking about how I'm not free, and I haven't helped you be free.

"And who knows whether Lucia's living the life she wanted or maybe she's not even alive! Why didn't we try harder to find out what happened to her? Why didn't I send your father to the farm where she went to work to ask if anyone had seen her? Why didn't I go there myself? I have many regrets, many regrets about what I didn't do, about what I didn't learn to do."

I began to weep. Tears pooled on my chin and dripped onto my shawl. Verónica knelt beside me and put her arms around me. My chest was moving up and down from crying. In that moment, I felt like giving up our experiment. I think that Verónica was worried I might give up because she held me tight and wouldn't let me go.

I let her hold me for awhile after I stopped crying. Then I pulled myself up straight and gently removed her arm from around my shoulders. I smiled to let her know I was better. "Daughter, listen to me because I'm going to tell you something I never told you before. I'm going to tell you about how bad things were for me, your father, and Lucia the year you were born. And something I almost did because I was really afraid."

"Alright, Mother," Verónica said. "But first I want to tell you that you aren't just a woman of the mountains. You know a lot. You know how to tell a person's life story so we can understand how they felt, why they did what they did. When Lucia's story is done, you and I will be authors. Just think! Your words will be in a book! You'll be famous!"

I chuckled. "You know that books don't matter to me. But I'm glad that I can help you and I won't abandon our experiment. Sometimes I just have to tell you how all this talking makes me feel. Now, let me talk again!

We both laughed. "Alright, Mother, I'm listening!"

Well, the year you were born was a good year for Lucia because she wasn't drinking anymore, and many people asked her to pray for them. Word had gotten around about how the co-op store was doing well after she prayed for it. People even came all the way from Chamula to ask her to pray, but she didn't want to leave her mother so she only prayed in Lokan and nearby communities.

Your father and I took our turn at the store along with the other co-op members. It was a sacrifice because we had to leave your brothers at home by themselves. But Abolino and Sebastian were in school by then, and when they came home in the afternoon they knew how to help themselves to tortillas and beans. I hated for them to eat alone, but it was what we had to do.

I said there were beans, but in truth during those years we usually ran out of beans many months before the next harvest. When we didn't have money to buy beans, we just ate tortillas and greens with a little salt. I know that greens are good for you, but in those years when we had only greens to put inside our tortillas we felt no better than cows.

Around this time, we started to plant coffee because we heard that we could sell it at a good price and with that money buy the beans we couldn't produce ourselves. I also started to sell my weavings through a co-op that wasn't part of the government. From that day until today selling coffee and weavings has been the only way we've been able to survive.

For a long time before you were born, your father went away for months at a time to make money to buy what we couldn't grow. He built roads. He cut sugar cane and took care of cattle on a ranch one year. He never left Chiapas, but little by little they stopped building roads and other things. Your father and other men from Lokan didn't have any way to make money. We still had land to plant milpa, but not enough to grow all the food we needed. Now that your brothers have their inheritance there's even less, and they can barely feed their families. But I'm getting ahead of myself.

The year before you were born, when the coffee harvest came in, we could only get a few pesos for it. The price had dropped so much that we wondered why we had bothered to plant it. With the few pesos we earned from selling our coffee, we could only buy beans for a couple months. Your father talked about going to find work in Veracruz or Cancún. But he had a cargo in the Word of God, and we depended on him to do his turn at the co-op store.

Not long after your father talked about going away to work, I found out that I was pregnant. I felt desperate because I didn't think we could feed another mouth. When we ran out of corn, I ground up a root and made a dough like masa to make tortillas.

The night that I told your father I was pregnant, I didn't know what he would say. I didn't know if he would be happy and say we didn't need to worry, or if he would be sad like me.

He was worried, and so we talked about what we could do. We talked about getting an abortion, even though the padres and madres didn't approve of it. Since they weren't married and didn't have children, we didn't take their words about having babies into our hearts.

We made a plan to go to a clinic where a promotora who spoke tsotsil did abortions. I didn't know if it was the right thing to do. For many nights before the day we were to go, I couldn't sleep. I kept wondering if the Virgin Mary would be angry with me for not having my baby. I prayed to her to forgive me. But I also wondered what kind of a child my baby would be, would it be a girl or a boy, would it look like me or your father? If it was a girl, would she want me to teach her to weave when she got bigger?

I woke up extra early the morning we were to go to the clinic and went into the kitchen to make tortillas. When your father came in, he found me crying while I was turning the last of the tortillas on the comal.

He sat down by the fire and put his head in his hands. I was still crying when I said, "I've been thinking that we don't have as many children as most families and we only have boys. You know what the ancestors say, that mothers are guardians of their sons' souls and fathers of their daughters' souls. I have two sons' souls to care for, but you don't have even one daughter's. I think we need to have our child, in case it's a girl. Even if it's not, we'll have another son to help you in the fields and to bring more happiness into our home.

Your father kept his head in his hands while I talked and didn't look up for a long time, or at least it seemed so. Finally, he said, "You're right. Our family isn't that big. We can feed this baby. God will help us. I've always wanted a daughter and even if we don't have one, another son will be good too."

So it was settled, and we went on as if we'd never thought of not having you. Your birth was easier than when I had your two brothers. When I first saw you and then during the six days we rested together on our separate bed near the fire, I felt sure that I had done the right thing. You were a very pretty baby. You had the same long eyelashes you have now and the same reddish color in your hair when the sun hits it. I felt content that now your father had a child's soul to care for, and I had a daughter to teach how to weave.

And look at you now! You're a good weaver, and you're learning how to write people's stories."

Verónica didn't look pleased at my compliment. She turned off the tape recorder and seemed to be searching for words. Finally she said, "I'm trying to imagine not being wanted or not even being alive! I need some time to think about how I almost didn't come to be."

I felt sorry for Verónica and wanted to help her accept what I'd told her, so I said, "Remember how it was the year you lived with Rodrigo? You wouldn't have wanted a baby with him. You were so poor. Rodrigo hardly brought you any corn or beans, and he was cruel to you. How could you have had a baby when you couldn't even feed yourself? That's how your father and I felt."

"It's true, I'm glad I didn't have a baby when I lived with Rodrigo. Some day I would like to have one though. But for now my job is keeping me busy."

Verónica was quiet. I didn't know what to say, so I told her I wanted to continue telling about the problems and conflicts in Chenalhó at that time. She nodded and turned on the tape recorder.

The same year you were born, a group of Catholics in the northern part of Chenalhó got together and started the Civil Society of the Bees, which we just called the Bees. They never use arms to protest. Instead they used words and marches to sting the government like bees to make it listen to injustices.

We had a lot of tensions during those years between the religious ones and the different political parties. When the Bees first got together, there were disagreements about who owned a gravel pit. Some people died during that time. Now we know that the bad government was trying to manipulate people by giving them money so they'd stay quiet and helping men arm themselves and form paramilitary groups to crush the people who want justice.

Lucia and I found out about the Bees when we went to the courses in Yabteclum and after your father came back from meetings of the Believers where there were many Bees. Your father's sisters married men who were Bees. Your aunt Ernestina married a Bee too. That's why none of them are Zapatistas. But we support one another, our organizations are united.

During this time I was mostly thinking about my family and my weavings, not much about the troubles going on. Lucia was thinking about prayers and healing plants and also trying to keep herself and her mother fed by working in others' fields. But she was always a little sad.

I missed her smile and hearty laugh. We still visited back and forth. Lucia always brought us lemongrass because none grew near our house. Your brothers loved lemongrass tea, and you giggled with joy when Lucia came to visit. She'd bounce you up and down on her lap and carry you around in her shawl, just like you were her own child.

Then one night, one cold night in 1993—I know the year because it was in December just before the struggle began—Lucia had a dream. She was always dreaming and telling me about her dreams, but this dream was different. It was another cargo dream, like the one she had when she was a little girl. But we didn't know it at the time. We just knew that Lucia had to pay attention to it and wait to find out what it meant.

Your father had gone to get firewood, you and your brothers were still sleeping, and I was making tortillas like I am right now when Lucia came running down the path. She paused outside the door, just long enough to ask if I was home.

Then she rushed in, which wasn't like her, and sat abruptly on the chair beside me. I could see that she had something urgent to say,

"What is it, Comadre? Did something happen?"

She took a deep breath and said, "Yes, something happened. Do you remember the dream I had when I was little? Well, the Moon Virgin came to me again."

"She did?" I was surprised and a little envious.

"Yes, she did. She did. In my dream I was still sleeping, but I woke up when a bright light filled the space around my bed. The Moon Virgin stood inside the light, holding out her arms to me. Then she started to talk to me.

'She said, 'Daughter, I've seen that you're not drinking. My heart is happy that you gave up pox and that you're doing good work on Earth. But I can see that you're still sad. I don't want you to be sad. I believe in you. You're my daughter. That's why I've come to tell you that your work has just begun. I've come to call you to do new work for me and for all the Believers on Earth. Don't be afraid. I'll take care of you. I'll give you strength because you're my chosen child. Just be patient and pray. Talk to me. Soon your work will be revealed to you.'"

THE TIME OF STRUGGLE

I HAD JUST FINISHED TELLING VERÓNICA about Lucia's dream when we heard Victorio unloading firewood. I could see that Verónica didn't want to stop our work, but I always stopped what I was doing when Victorio came home from chopping wood or working in the fields. I respected how hard he worked and didn't want to take him for granted. So I gave him his food and matz and sat down and talked with him.

"Let's continue later today," I told Verónica. "I need to finish the ceremonial blouse I've been working on."

Verónica muttered something that I couldn't hear and went to help a neighbor who had come to the store. She wasn't happy, but what could I do? I had a deadline to enter the blouse in a competition.

I made a lot of progress that afternoon. After the three pieces of the blouse were done, I ran my hands over the many small red diamonds that covered half of the front of the blouse. Later, when Verónica came in to see how I was doing, she had forgotten her anger and liked what she saw.

"It's beautiful!" she said. "When you weave, you're not afraid to experiment or recover old things that people have forgotten or don't care about anymore."

I was encouraged by my daughter's words and thought I would teach her a little bit about the blouse. So I asked, "Did you know that these pieces have names?"

"No, what are their names?"

"Well, they say that the middle piece is called 'its mother' and the side pieces are called 'its arms.' It's a living thing, you know. When a woman wears it, she stands in the center of the universe where the ancient ceiba tree stood. There she has power to speak to the saints, God, and all the spiritual beings on behalf of our people."

"That's what it says in my book of designs too!" Verónica was excited that her book and my stories were the same.

"We can talk now," I told her. "I'm going to sew the pieces together tomorrow."

"What are you going to talk about today, Mother?" she asked.

"I'm going to tell you about the time of struggle."

"What do you mean? Hasn't Lucia's life been one long struggle?"

Verónica couldn't imagine more struggle than she had already heard me talk about, but I explained that the struggle I was about to describe was not just Lucia's, but the struggle of many people.

"Oh, so you're going to tell me about when the Zapatistas rose up against the government in 1994 when I was just two years old. I can't count the number of times I've heard about the day the Zapatistas arrived in Lokan, Mother! You've told me a million times how they gathered the Believers together to explain that they were indigenous people too, that they had been organizing for many years far away in the jungles of Chiapas, and that everyone needed to work together to make the bad government listen to our demands. I don't want to hear the basics again! I want to hear more details."

"Daughter, trust me. I'm not going to tell you that again. No. I'm going to tell you about what happened when Lucia and I joined the Zapatistas and how our lives changed after that."

"All right, Mother. That's something I don't know about."

My shawl was tightly drawn across my chest, and my arms were folded around my waist when Verónica returned with her tape recorder and notebook. I think I looked like a butterfly wrapped up in a cocoon as I told my daughter about becoming a Zapatista.

I was at home with you on January 1st when my mother stopped by after going to San Cristóbal to buy some thread.

She looked scared and began to talk in a very agitated way even before she sat down.

She said, "When I got off the bus in San Cristóbal the streets were silent. I couldn't find anyone to buy thread from. I tried to stop a Chamula woman who was running with a load of charcoal on her back, but she didn't stop when I asked her where all the people were. She just cried out, 'They're killing people in San Cristóbal, there's a war going on! Get back to your homes as fast as you can!'

"I became very worried and ran back to the market to find a ride to Lokan. On the way home, many people were talking about what they had heard. They said that a group of people called Zapatistas stormed into the city hall at dawn and threw all the papers over the balcony onto the street. They shouted many things from the balcony, but no one knew what they said. They were dressed all in black, and they wore masks and some carried guns. Others carried sticks made to look like guns. And some of them were women dressed in pants just like men!

"Daughter, I don't understand this. What does it mean? Will it come to Lokan?"

I made my mother some chamomile tea to calm her down. She was very agitated. I felt nervous too, thinking about what she had told me. I wished that Victorio was home so he could help us understand what was happening. But he might not know any more than we did.

After your grandmother had finished her tea, she said she needed to go home to tell your grandfather. So she left me there nursing you and trying not to worry about what was happening.

Your father came home early with half a load of firewood because someone had told him what was happening in San Cristóbal. While we were talking about what we knew, a neighbor came to tell us that there was a meeting in the church about the situation. So your father got his hat and left quickly. I stayed by the fire with you waiting for your brothers to come home from school. I didn't want to be alone in those moments of fear, with many, many questions.

It wasn't long before we had answers. Just two days later a group of Zapatistas came to Lokan to tell us who they were and why they had taken up arms. They invited everyone to the meeting, even women and boys and girls over fifteen years old. Many people came from neighboring communities.

I went with your father and listened to everything. Not just Zapatista men came to talk with us. Women came too. Lucia sat with her mother, my parents, and me. Not many Presbyterians or Evangelicals came. They said that they didn't have to struggle on earth for salvation, because it was waiting for them in heaven. But it didn't take long before some of them understood why we have to struggle on earth, and they joined us.

I know you don't want to hear everything the Zapatista representatives said. But I can tell you that it was as if they were saying the things that we had been guarding in our hearts without saying them. We decided that we had to join them.

They told us that we could gather ourselves together and form a support base. At our first meeting we would elect representatives, equal numbers of women and men. Four men and four women. I remember Lucia and I looked at each other when we heard this because we couldn't think of even one woman who could take a cargo. Everyone was too busy with many children to take care of.

Next they told us that we would receive information from the Zapatista leaders from time to time, and we would meet to talk about it in terms of what made sense and was important to us.

Their way of working was a lot like how the madres taught us to read the Bible: to consider what the words say about our lives and then act on what we thought was right. Word of God meetings were like support bases, so it didn't seem that different, what the Zapatistas described.

Most of us didn't know about guns, though, but the Zapatistas explained that we would not be armed. Instead we would focus on the needs in our communities by organizing economic projects. This way we would no longer be dependent on government handouts.

We immediately knew what they were talking about because the Believers had already run a cooperative store. I belonged to a weaving group. We were already in the resistance, we just didn't call it that.

On the way home Lucia and I talked about the requirement to have both women and men representatives. I was really worried about it and told Lucia so.

"How could any woman in Lokan be a representative? Almost everyone is married with young children. Only a single woman or a widow would have time to attend meetings. But young women don't know that much yet and lack experience and wisdom. And many widows never went to school and don't speak Spanish. It would help if the representative knows a little Spanish. Can you think of anyone who could be a good representative?"

"You would be, Comadre," Lucia said.

"Me? How could I do that with my work in the weaving co-op and all my responsibilities at home?'

"I know it would be hard. I just said this because you're wise and have experience organizing cooperatives."

"How about you, Lucia? You're very intelligent, and you have a lot of experience settling problems through prayer. You speak Spanish well. People respect you."

"But you know how I was in the past. Maybe the work will be too hard for me, and I'll fall again."

"But you've been sober for a long time. And you won't be the only woman representative. We'll choose other single woman, and if they're younger than you, you can help them learn how to lead. You'll have important work to do."

"We're talking here like we're the committee to choose the women representatives!" Lucia said. We laughed. We realized we were jumping way ahead of the process that we would have to follow to choose the women representatives. It would have to be democratic. Everything we would do from that time on had to be democratic.

The day for the meeting to choose our representatives came, and there were a lot of people there, about sixty or seventy, mostly men. About twenty women came. We knew almost everyone because of how our families have intermarried. Lucia and I looked around, and we could see that there were only two or maybe three women who might be willing to take a cargo as representative.

Your father started the nomination process. I had already told him that in no way would I consider being a representative. He had already suggested Lucia, and I agreed. Now it was up to the whole group to decide who our representatives would be.

We took a long time that afternoon to come to an agreement. To my horror I was nominated! I had to tell everyone that I had too many responsibilities to take a cargo, but that I would attend meetings and support the base in every way I could. The people accepted my explanation, but they didn't seem happy about it.

The next person nominated was Lucia. When her name was announced she looked a little worried, but she spoke in a confident voice. "I accept the nomination. I would be honored to serve my people in this way. If I'm chosen it may be a little hard for me being a healer and having to help my mother, but I will do my best."

Everyone nodded. It was as if a big sigh of relief came up from the people gathered there. Everyone could see that it was going to be very hard to find four women representatives, and that we might have to be satisfied with only two.

There was a long silence until finally Lucia raised her hand and nominated a young woman named Ramona. I knew her from the courses at Yabteclum. I had told Lucia about her because she had taken over reading the Bible verses like Lucia had done before her. Ramona showed a lot of respect to people. Thanks to God, Ramona accepted. Then we voted on the two women, and it was unanimous. Everyone accepted Lucia and Ramona as our first women representatives in the support base.

Then four men were nominated and voted on. That was easy as many men wanted to serve. Your father was chosen to be one of the representatives. We also chose a young man, Ángel de Jesús, who was active in the Word of God with your father and me. I was glad about all our choices, because even though I couldn't be a representative, I knew that Victorio and Lucia would tell me everything that was going on, and I could help them with any problems that might come up.

On our way home from the meeting Lucia walked with us. Before we parted, I took her hand and said, "It has come, Comadre, the time that the Moon Virgin foretold in your dream. Your cargo has been revealed to you, the way you will serve our people, the people of Chiapas, and the world."

Lucia opened her eyes wide as if to take in the meaning of my words. She put her other hand on mine and said, "Comadre, will you help me? I will need your help and my compadre's help too."

Your father heard Lucia and said, "Comadre, we'll do everything together. You won't be alone."

ÁNGEL DE JESÚS

VERÓNICA WANTED ME TO TALK ABOUT what it was like when the Mexican army came to Chenalhó and set up roadblocks and bases. She doesn't remember those years because she was still little. Just before she asked me to talk about this time, she found a box of our families' things under my bed, and in it were some drawings that Abolino and Sebastian had made after the uprising. On those tattered sheets of paper were the things that had frightened people so much, seen through the eyes of my sons, still in primary school.

They had drawn helicopters whirling over the heads of terrified people; a convoy of tanks, like giant ants moving along the road below our house; soldiers poking their helmet-covered heads through the holes in the top of the tanks. My sons also drew crowds of Zapatistas on the road confronting the tanks, shaking their fists at them and saying, "We don't want you here!" They put the people's words in bubbles above their heads like in comic books.

Sebastian made a lot of drawings of Zapatistas with ski masks and leaping in the air like ninjas! Abolino seemed to be most interested in drawing pictures of Subcommander Marcos smoking his pipe and saying things like, "Never again a Mexico without us!" At that time my sons didn't understand much about Marcos or the Zapatistas or what it meant that we didn't feel that we were a part of Mexico, but they were excited to have some action come to Lokan.

I've never shown much interest in my children's drawings. It's true. I always told my children, "If you want a picture of something, take a photo of it." Of course we don't have a camera, so that left my children with only drawings. But when Verónica took her brothers' drawings out of the box and laid them on the table, they took me immediately back to the time of struggle.

Verónica pointed to a drawing of a tank and asked me if I remembered it. I nodded. Then she showed me one of Sebastian's Zapatista ninjas. She burst out laughing at the drawing. When I didn't laugh too, she asked me what was wrong.

"Nothing. I'm just remembering something, a very sad thing that happened to some boys."

"Tell me, Mother. What boys? What happened to them?"

I laid the drawing on top of the others and looked into the fire and told her about what happened in 1996.

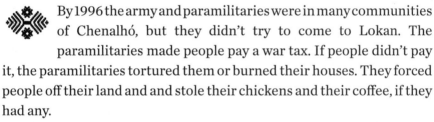 By 1996 the army and paramilitaries were in many communities of Chenalhó, but they didn't try to come to Lokan. The paramilitaries made people pay a war tax. If people didn't pay it, the paramilitaries tortured them or burned their houses. They forced people off their land and and stole their chickens and their coffee, if they had any.

We began to hear about refugee camps with hundreds of families suffering in the cold and rain. Many rumors of different kinds about suffering and violence spread throughout the township. Some of them seemed impossible to believe, but still I wondered if they could be true. Like the one about headcutters, men dressed all in black who came into houses or attacked people on the path and cut their heads off with machetes! Some said that they carried ropes to tie people up.

When we heard these rumors, we were terrified to walk at night on the paths. Lucia never stopped going to people's houses to pray for them, but she was afraid too. To protect herself, she always carried wild tobacco with her. Thank God, nothing happened to Lucia or to any of our family or compañeros.

But something terrible happened that summer to seven young men who were staying at a hotel in the lum. We never found out exactly who they were, but it seems that they were just boys, studying and living together somewhere outside of San Cristóbal. I don't know why they were in Chenalhó. Someone said they saw them leaping off of the bridge into the river, all dressed in black, like those ninjas in Sebastian's drawings.

Many rumors started about them, but the one that led to their deaths accused them of being headcutters. One night a mob of people from the lum who believed this rumor went to the hotel and grabbed the boys out of their beds. They tied them up and carried them a long way from town to a deep crevice in the side of the mountain where the highway passes. I still shudder when I pass that spot because that's where they threw the seven boys and left them there to die.

"Mother, how horrible. How terrible for the families of the boys, Verónica said."

"Yes, many mothers were sad because of their sons. Not only mothers of boys who were killed, but mothers of boys who killed others. We couldn't understand how boys who had grown up learning to help their fathers in the fields and to speak in the high voice to elders, could take a gun and kill someone! But that's what happened. We heard that the men who trained the boys gave them these drugs that make people act crazy. We heard that they showed them films about men killing people and then eating a big meal together right after."

"Oh, Mother, I'm so glad that Abolino and Sebastian didn't do anything horrible like that."

"No, thank God. As soon as Abolino turned fifteen, he joined the support base. In the base he started to learn about the struggle. The representatives gave him and the other young men cargos as sentries.

Abolino learned what a cargo was that year because he really suffered. Each night, at about 9 p.m., he would leave the house with a blanket and climb about a mile to a lookout spot on the mountain. Another young man who had the same cargo joined him. They took turns guarding and sleeping. They watched for strangers or men who looked like paramilitaries. They never saw any, but they were doing important work for us, guarding our community from possible threats.

About 4 a.m., Abolino and I would pass each other in the kitchen where I was starting to make tortillas. He came to drink his matz before joining Sebastian under the blankets to catch a few hours of sleep.

"Mother, now I remember something about that time! Early in the morning, after you would get up, I remember Abolino would get into bed. I was still half asleep, and it seemed like a dream. Until now, I didn't know that Abolino had a cargo when he was still a boy. It seems that everyone had cargos when they were growing up except me!

"Tell me more about Lucia's second cargo, Mother. How could she accept it on top of her work as a healer? I guess Lucia also wondered, or she wouldn't have asked you and Father for help."

When I continued, I told Verónica how Lucia was able to manage her cargo for a while, because the Moon Virgin sent her a helper.

"Oh, you mean Ramona, the other woman representative?"

"No. Not Ramona. It wasn't her. It was Ángel de Jesús."

"How strange," she said. "What made Ángel de Jesús want to help Lucia?"

"Well, that's a long story," I chuckled. "But I guess that's what I'm doing here, telling long stories."

"Yes, Mother, so keep going!"

Well, one afternoon Lucia came over, and we talked about the problems with men in the base who didn't want to stop drinking. She told me about a meeting the week before when some of the men proposed a punishment for base members who refused to give up pox.

As you know, to be a Zapatista, a person can't drink. But Lucia didn't like the punishment the men wanted to give the drinkers. First, they would give the man a warning, with a talk about how pox keeps people from thinking clearly. Then if the man still didn't stop, they would give a second warning, with a stronger talk—a scolding.

Then if the person still kept drinking, they would go to his home early in the morning and take him to a tree near the church. They would tie him to the tree and leave him for about four or five hours. I guess the idea was to give him plenty of time to think about the error of his ways. While he was tied to the tree, his family could bring him food and water.

Lucia was very angry about the men's idea. She thought the punishment was cruel. She told me, "If the men tied me to a tree, it would make me so furious I would leave the base. What right do the men have to shame a person so? Anyway, even if the person stopped drinking afterwards, it wouldn't last. They would go back to drinking. You can't force someone to stop drinking. Their hearts have to want to stop and they need time to change."

I nodded in agreement. Lucia had taught me a lot about what it takes to stop drinking. She continued. "At the meeting, Ángel de Jesús kept his head lowered and looked at the floor while the men talked. A few times he raised his head and looked over at me as if he wanted me to say something. But I didn't know what to say. The punishment shocked me. When they asked me what I thought, I said I would have to think about it. They also asked Ángel de Jesús and he said what I said, but so softly I could barely hear him.

"Early the next morning I heard Ángel de Jesús coming down the path toward my house. He was calling to me in the bik'it snuk' as he approached the door. I smiled to hear the high voice spoken to me and welcomed Ángel de Jesús into the kitchen. From the way he fingered the rim of his hat, I could see that there was something on his mind. Mother had gone to the market and wouldn't be back until afternoon. So fortunately we had time to talk. Ángel de Jesús sat down and told me what was on his mind."

"'Older sister, I have something to tell you,' he said. "'I know I can trust you because you're an j'ilol, and you drank in the past. You lost your soul, but you got it back. Now you're even stronger than before, and everyone respects you. You deserve to be a Zapatista representative, and so do the other representatives.

"'But I don't deserve this cargo. I'm not worthy of it. You see, I'm still drinking. I drink at home, so only my parents know. They don't say anything because they hope that my cargo in the base will help me stop drinking. But no cargo is going to make me stop. I'm drinking because I need courage to be myself. Drinking helps me forget that I don't fit in Lokan. There's no place for a man like me here.'"

"What do you mean?" I asked. I wasn't being completely honest with Ángel de Jesús because I had an idea what he meant. I'd been aware of him for a while, even before he joined the base.

"Once when I was coming home from a healing just as night was falling, I heard a rustling sound in the trees. I hurried along, but when I was a ways down the path, curiosity made me glance back. Although it was dark, I saw two young men walk onto the trail and embrace. They were saying goodbye in the way lovers do, not wanting to let the other go. One of them was Ángel de Jesús. I had never known an antsil vinik in Lokan, but it seemed that he and the other man were like that.

"When I saw Ángel with his lover, a feeling of relief flooded over me. Although I didn't know a woman in Lokan who loved another woman, I now knew there were at least two men who loved each other. I let Ángel de Jesús tell me what I already knew, even though it was very hard for him."

"'You probably wonder why I'm not married, since I'm almost twenty-three,'" Ángel de Jesús said. "'It's because I can't imagine marrying. I've never been attracted to women. When my friends used to tell me that they wanted a girl, I didn't understand them. Instead, I wanted them! I know this must sound strange to you. You must think the Earthlord has my soul and is making me the opposite of what I should be. But my soul isn't lost. It's not lost. It's not the Earthlord's prisoner. My soul is well-seated inside me. I'm just not like other men in Lokan.'"

"When he finished, Ángel de Jesús lowered his head, waiting for me to say something. 'I don't think you're strange,' I said. 'As a healer I have been inside hundreds of homes, and I know how many different kinds of people we live amongst. But also, I accept who you are because I understand how you feel. You see, I never married because I'm a woman who doesn't want to be with a man.

'I only want to be with a woman, but here in Lokan that's not possible. It's taboo. I drank to manage my sadness. I almost killed myself because I couldn't accept living without my heart's desire.

'I still wonder what my life could be like if I had the freedom that comes with living in the city. There must be people like us who go to San Cristóbal where no one will care who they love. You're a man, people would understand if you went to San Cristóbal to work.

'I hear there are Zapatista bases there so you wouldn't have to leave the organization. There's also something called Alcoholics Anonymous— groups of people who help each other stop drinking through talking and prayer.'

After Lucia finished, Ángel de Jesús told her that he was afraid to live in the city because his brother was murdered in Cancún. He went with his parents to bring his brother's body back to Chiapas. When he was in the city, he felt as if it would swallow him up, like it did his brother. After that, he never wanted to live anywhere but Lokan.

Lucia tried to think of how to advise him. But nothing came to her at the time. Instead she told Ángel that she would pray a special prayer to help him stop drinking. He seemed relieved. Then Lucia told me that that night Ángel had a dream.

"Ángel's dream combined the dream I had when the Moon Virgin came to give me my cargo to be an j'ilol, and the one I had about eight years ago when she came to help me stop drinking. When Ángel told me about his dream, I worried that the Virgin was asking too much of him, to learn to be a healer while he was still drinking. Maybe she thought he could do it because I was there to help him. After all, she had called me her chosen child. Chosen for what, I often asked myself? To help others, I concluded."

The morning of the prayer, Ángel de Jesús met Lucia at the chapel. He brought three bottles of soda, candles, incense, and pine boughs. Lucia prayed with her whole heart for Ángel de Jesús. I think she had become fond of him because he reminded her of herself.

Lucia told me that she had to pray two more times for Ángel de Jesús, but that she had a good feeling about what the outcome would be. I attended a meeting of the whole base soon after the third prayer and was pleased to hear Ángel speak in a confident voice. Many people nodded in agreement, because his words made good sense. Later Lucia told me that she was teaching Ángel to pray and heal with herbs. It seemed that his heart really wanted to change because he was enthusiastic and learning fast.

So that's the story of Ángel de Jesús. Now thirteen years later, he's still with us, healing and serving his cargo in the base. He says that his cargo is his glass of water, that it quenches his thirst for justice. He says that Jesús and Zapata walk on each side of him, giving him their strength. But he always seems a little sad to me. I think he misses Lucia because they went everywhere together.

Verónica was quiet after I finished. Then she said, "Why don't I know about Ángel and Lucia? There's so much I don't know! So many stories exist in a place like Lokan. I'm really glad you told me these stories, Mother. Listening to you I feel like the archaeologist on TV, uncovering layer after layer of an ancient Maya city."

It was time to put the corn on to boil and prepare for bed. After we were done in the kitchen, Verónica followed me outside into the dark patio but didn't come into the sleeping house with me. The sky was filled with stars, and she was looking up at them. As I folded the clothes on my side of the bed to make a little pillow, I looked through the half-open door to see if Verónica was coming. But she hadn't moved. She was still looking up at the sky.

WHEN A WOMAN RISES

WE HAD COME TO THE LAST CHAPTER in my story of Lucia. Verónica and I couldn't believe that more than eight months had passed since our first talks. It was now early June, and the rains had started. Back in November when we began, Verónica was afraid of her tape recorder and of erasing my words by accident. But she shouldn't have been. Lucia's story was engraved in both our hearts, and nothing could erase it.

Rain was coming down hard the day we finished Lucia's story. When it hit the metal roof, it sounded like bullets. Not that we'd ever heard bullets, but I imagine if we did they would sound that way. Since the beginning of the struggle, the Zapatistas and the Bees have been trying to keep arms out of Lokan and they've succeeded. But we haven't been spared the sadness of losing friends who died in the struggle in other communities.

I'll never forget December 1997. I remember that Lucia had only been gone a few weeks when bullets rained down without mercy on forty-five women, men, and children in a chapel in Acteal, a community about an hour from Lokan. The people who perished that day were Bees, and they were in a chapel praying for peace when they died. Many children died that day. I still can't understand how men, not that different from the ones in our community, could have killed their neighbors. We know that the bad government gave guns to a paramilitary group called the Red Mask and taught them to kill, but that still doesn't explain how the men could have separated themselves so far from their souls. When we heard that the soldiers at the military post could hear the shooting and did nothing, we were even more horrified.

Verónica and I were both a little sad and nervous waiting for the rain to stop and to record the end of Lucia's story. Our special time together was ending, and now Verónica had to write up what she had learned from me. I wouldn't be able to help her with the writing part. She would be alone from now on. I thought to myself that I hope Verónica learned from Lucia's story to be strong and believe in herself.

I pushed my fears down and tried to think of this day as just another day of talking about Lucia. Verónica looked in her notebook for remaining questions. After she didn't find any, she signaled me to begin.

By the end of the first year of her cargo, Lucia was really struggling to pay her transportation to Zapatista meetings in Polhó and to help her mother out as she worked in other people's fields. Your father and I loaned her money when we had it, and I'm sure other people did too.

She was still praying for people and getting a little food and money that way. She also started embroidering squares of cloth designed with women Zapatistas wearing bandanas over their faces and working in the fields with babies on their backs. On the cloth she embroidered words like, "When a woman rises, no man is left behind." She earned a little money selling her squares to foreigners who came to Polhó to learn about the Zapatistas and find out how to show their solidarity.

But it seemed that every time I saw Lucia she looked thinner and more tired. The base members thought that it would be easier for single women to be representatives. We were thinking of single women living with two parents and perhaps several siblings, like Ramona. Ramona had five brothers. In contrast, Lucia only had her mother.

One night about a year after we joined the Zapatista base, I talked to your father about how hard it was for Lucia to be a representative. I didn't expect what happened. We had an argument! Maybe you don't remember us yelling at each other, but I'm sure your brothers do.

All I said to your father was that Lucia and her mother could barely maintain themselves and that made it really hard for Lucia to serve a cargo. I said that except for Ramona and Lucia, our community had no other single women who felt comfortable taking on a big job for the community. I added that all the married women have too much to do to take on extra work. Then I said that if men helped their wives cook, wash clothes, or take care of the children maybe then women could serve cargos.

I finished by saying that wives help their husbands in the fields, but husbands don't help their wives in the house. Even though I was pointing out the obvious, your father didn't like what I said and got angry. He raised his voice and said, "What are you saying? That I don't help you?"

I answered, "That's not what I'm saying exactly, but it's true that you don't do as much as you could."

Then your father said, "But how can I do more? I'm already barely home with all the meetings and working in the fields. And even if I was home more, I can't do the things you do. They're women's work. My father taught me men's work. You know that. Now you want to change everything overnight!"

Your father's face turned reddish brown and the scar on his face stood out like a bolt of lightening on a dark cloud. He wouldn't look at me. I tried to calm him down and still get my point across. I said to him, "It's not just me. It's the organization. They say that things have got to change, so women can be leaders too. You know I have a lot to say and so do the other women. You've seen how we can analyze the word of God and then act on it in our lives. Can't you see that we just want to keep growing?"

Your father looked really angry, like he wanted to hit me. Thank God, he didn't. Maybe he stopped himself because he didn't want to have to say a prayer asking for forgiveness for arguing in front of our children!

Neither of us said anything for a while. You children just drank your matz in silence. I tried to contain my anger, but I couldn't control myself completely. Instead of yelling at your father, I slammed the lid down hard on the pot of boiling corn.

Your father got up without speaking and began to gather his hoe and other things he needed to take to the milpa. I pressed a ball of matz into his hands. He accepted it, but he didn't look at me. Then he told the boys to get ready to go to the fields. They had a lot of weeding to do, he said.

Later that day your father returned from the milpa as usual, but then he did something he had never done. He took off his pants and shirt and went behind the house to the rocks near the rotoplas. While I worked on my loom, I listened to the sound of water sloshing furiously over clothes! Then your father hung his shirt and pants out to dry on the line in front of our house.

I didn't say anything about what he had done until we were in bed that night. Before we fell asleep, I thanked him for washing his clothes. He turned toward the wall and grunted, "You're welcome."

I paused and Verónica said, "I've always wondered why Father washes his own clothes when many men don't. I thought it was because they don't have a rotoplas like us and are embarrassed to wash at the water hole where only women and children go. But now I know that you could defend your rights and other women's too."

"I don't know if I defended myself so much. But, yes, somehow we women managed to do all our work and still be Zapatistas. Looking back, I don't know how I did it. During the early years of the organization, you were still a little girl and couldn't help me much. But I was young and had more energy. I could do more in a day back then."

Not long after our discussion that day, your father began to help me in different ways, not only washing clothes. I think that the example he set for your brothers encouraged them to help their wives. Today they help a lot in the house and with their children, compared to how it was in the beginning with your father. I'm just glad that men and women are more equal now.

For a while Lucia could fulfill her duties with Ángel's help. He was like her assistant, not just in her work for the base, but in her healing. They were like siblings who went everywhere together.

Soon people began to say that Ángel was Lucia's kexol, her replacement. I was one of the first to say it, because I watched how Lucia was preparing Ángel to take her place. I don't think she even knew she was doing it. But the Moon Virgin knew. I think that she chose Ángel to replace Lucia because she knew Lucia wouldn't be with us very long. The Moon gently helped Lucia transfer her gifts to Ángel. When we finally accepted that Lucia was not coming back, Ángel became Lucia's official replacement. Little by little he earned the authority to speak during meetings on behalf of women, as well as men.

One day in October of 1997, Lucia came to tell me that she was going away for a while. I couldn't believe my ears. My whole body became cold. She said she had to go away to make some money. She was going to Sinaloa to work on a tomato farm, just like her father had done. She assured me that she wouldn't go to the same farm where he had gone and that she wouldn't be gone long, just until Holy Week. I counted in my head, five months.

While Lucia was talking, I wanted to ask her, "But what about the rule that Zapatistas aren't supposed to migrate for work? We need to stay here and help each other. Who are you going to find to take your cargo while you're gone?"

Lucia interrupted my thoughts. "Comadre, I know it's a lot to ask, but can you serve my cargo while I'm gone?"

I didn't say yes right away. Images flashed through my mind of traveling to meetings and sleeping on the ground far from home. I wondered how I could cover all my work at home and for the weaving co-op and the Zapatista co-op store if I was always in meetings.

I told Lucia yes, but not without a lot of effort. Lucia knew how much she was asking of me. But she wouldn't have left her cargo to work in Sinaloa if she had a choice.

That day Lucia began to tell me about the work I would have to do. Little by little, I accepted my new cargo. All the while I told myself that it was only for five months, and then it would be over. Looking back, those months were a blessing because they helped your father change into a man who could do women's work. He had no choice but to take over more of my work. He learned to cook and collect water. Once he began to do women's work, your father gained more respect for me and other women.

The news spread fast that Lucia was leaving. When Ricardo heard, he offered to give Carmela part of his corn and bean crop after harvest. The week before Lucia left, Ángel de Jesús announced at the base meeting that we would do a special prayer for Lucia so that her soul would follow her to Sinaloa. Lucia had taught him this prayer, the same one she prayed for us before we ran away to San Cristóbal.

That night I announced that four of the base representatives—

myself, Ramona, Ángel de Jesús, and your father—would fast for three days in Lucia's place. Normally, a person fasts before leaving to go to work far away. But Lucia was so thin that we feared if she were to fast she wouldn't have the strength for the journey and the hard work on the farm after she arrived.

I paused to adjust some logs on the fire. My hair wasn't in braids and covered much of my face as I bent over, so Verónica couldn't see the dark cloud that passed over me when I continued.

"You have seen me fast, daughter. I have fasted many times in my life for myself and others. Afterwards I have felt cleansed, peaceful, and of course, weak. But the time I fasted before Lucia's journey, something else happened, something terrifying."

The last night of my fast, I went to bed without having eaten anything for three days. I remember feeling dizzy and taking a long time to fall asleep. When my sleep finally came, it was deep and it revealed something horrible.

In my dream I was standing in a field dressed in men's clothes. My heart was beating fast and sweat was pouring off my body and making puddles on the ground. Maybe the puddles weren't sweat. Maybe they were my own urine because I couldn't control any part of my body. I couldn't even shut my eyes. I just stood there unable to look away from the most terrible thing I could imagine.

A woman stood in the center of a circle of flames, her face twisted in agony. Fire was consuming her clothes and turning her hair bright orange. Her flesh was falling off her bones. The poor woman was screaming in agony! But it wasn't just any woman. It was Lucia!

When I woke up from my nightmare, I was shaking from fear and hunger. I lifted myself from the bed with great difficulty. I wanted to tell your father about my dream, but he had been fasting too, and I thought it best to let him sleep.

So I went into the kitchen and drank a large gourd of water. I was so thirsty. Then I started to make tortillas, but my hands were shaking, and I couldn't make a decent one. I wanted to stop thinking about my nightmare, but I had to wait to tell it to your father and be rid of it forever. Or so I thought. I devoured my badly formed tortillas out of hunger. I was also ashamed for anyone to see them.

It seemed like a long time that I sat by the fire eating those tortillas and trying to make good ones for the family. Finally your father came into the kitchen and sat down. I gave him his matz and then told him about my nightmare. He listened without saying anything.

When I finished, he said, "The fire stands for something bad that will happen to Lucia. Maybe an enemy of the Zapatistas prayed to the Earth Lord to kill Lucia. We need to ask Ángel to pray for her as soon as possible."

I was still shaking when I said goodbye to Lucia that morning. Before she left, we gave each other a long embrace. After our bodies parted, she asked me why I was shaking, if I was sick. I didn't tell her about the nightmare. I just told her that I was cold.

I watched Lucia walk from our house to the road, a backpack and blanket strapped to her back. She was dressed in old pants and a blue shirt that your father gave her that morning. As she walked down the path, I thought how strange it was to see her legs encased in separate tubes of cloth. Her braids were tucked inside an old cap that Ángel had given her. Before she reached the road, one of her braids snaked its way out of the cap. She quickly stuffed it back.

For once I wished that the truck wouldn't be on time. But it was. Lucia climbed into the back and grabbed onto the overhead bar to steady herself. Seconds later she was gone. We didn't even have time to wave goodbye.

WE LEARN THE TRUTH

IT TOOK A COUPLE MONTHS for Verónica to transcribe my words and write up Lucia's story. She used three notebooks! She worked every day after making tortillas in the morning and after Victorio and I went to bed at night. The rest of the time she wove, did housework, helped me in our store, and went to meetings of the support base and the weaving co-op.

It was a Sunday night in early August when she was finally finished. She must have felt that she couldn't go back to life as usual, because she made a celebration. Monday morning she went to the lum and bought a cake mix and a jar of strawberry jam. Maruch, one of the Chamula girls she met in Telling Our Stories, told her how to make a cake in a frying pan in the coals.

After Verónica finished making tortillas, she spread out the coals and made a little bed for the frying pan. Then she filled the pan with the cake batter and covered it with a piece of a broken comal, so that the cake would cook all the way through, not only on the bottom. Her cake burned a little on the bottom, but the top was fine. She covered it with jam, set it on the table, and waited to see what I would say when I came home from my meeting.

"What's this?" I asked. I never thought I'd see a cake in our house because we don't have birthday parties like mestizos. Verónica explained that she wanted to celebrate finishing Lucia's story.

I gave a little sigh. So as not to disappoint Verónica, I offered to cut the cake. I cut it into four portions and put two aside. Verónica asked me why I cut the cake into forths instead of thirds, since there are only three of us in the house. Before I answered, Verónica realized that I had cut a piece for Lucia, as if I were putting out food for Lucia's soul on sk'in ch'ulelal.

To show Verónica I appreciated her new tradition, I made coffee, which we rarely drink since we only save a little for ourselves before we sell the rest. Verónica felt sick by the time she finished eating her piece of cake. She wasn't used to that much of a sweet thing! I ended up giving most of my piece to Victorio. Lucia's piece sat on the table uneaten.

The next day was another big day for Verónica. She had to go to San Cristóbal to deliver her story to Telling Our Stories. Diana wasn't in the office when she arrived, but she had left a note for Verónica and the other girls on the door. Verónica told me what it said.

"Dear compañeras,

I'm sorry I couldn't be here to receive your stories in person, but I had to attend a meeting at the last minute. I'm very excited to read your stories and look forward to talking with you about them at our meeting next week. Please just put your stories in the mail slot in the door.

Congratulations to all!

Strong hugs,

Diana

Verónica was actually relieved that she could just leave her story in the door because I had asked her to buy a little outfit in the market for Sebastian's new baby. I wanted to bring my grandson something pretty when I came to visit him for the first time. She picked out a little blue nightgown and cap and a fuzzy blue blanket with white satin ribbon on the border. A perfect present for my grandson.

When Verónica got back to Lokan that afternoon, Victorio and I were in the kitchen talking. As soon as she saw our faces, she asked what was wrong. We told her that a couple hours earlier a Chamula man had come looking for the family of Lucia Pérez López. Because our house is close to the road, he stopped here first.

We told him that Lucia's only family was her mother, and Victorio could take him to her house. When Victorio returned after leaving the man at Carmela's, he regretted not staying to hear the man's business. He said that the man didn't talk much on the way to Carmela's. He seemed to be on a mission and acted nervous. We were curious about who he was and why he wanted to talk to Carmela.

Victorio decided to see how Carmela was. Just as he started up the path he met the Chamula man coming back from Carmela's house. The man said that he had given Carmela some bad news and that she might need someone to talk to. Victorio asked the man what he had told Carmela, but the man said that that was for Carmela to tell us. Then he left quickly and Victorio increased his pace up the path to Carmela's house. Seconds later, I looked at Verónica and could see that we were thinking the same thing. We grabbed our shawls and hurried up the path until we caught up with Victorio.

As we neared Carmela's house, a cold feeling grabbed my body and stayed with me as I followed Victorio inside. Carmela was seated by the fire where I usually find her when I come to visit, but this day she was completely still, as if waiting for something or someone. Her hands lay open in her lap. Her body was hunched over, and she seemed to be looking for some answer inside her hands. But what could she be looking for? What did the man tell her that upset her so?

"Aunt," I said. "What happened? What message did the Chamula man bring? Was it from Lucia? Tell us so that we can know, so that you can unburden yourself."

Carmela raised her head slowly and looked at me with eyes that were red and puffy from crying. She stayed hunched over in the chair looking up at me until I came to sit beside her. I held her hand and said, "Aunt, tell us what the man told you. Whatever has made you so sad, we can bear it together."

Carmela put her hand on my knee. She seemed to want to speak, but nothing came out. I was patient, and tried not to press her. She finally spoke.

"The man brought me a great sadness, greater than I can bear. When Lucia's father disappeared, I thought it was the greatest sadness a woman could feel, losing her husband when she has a young child to raise. But, with Lucia to take care of, I adapted to Pedro being gone and accepted that whatever happened to him was God's will.

"When Lucia left, though, and never came back, it was harder to accept, perhaps because I was all alone. Maybe I also thought I'd find out someday what happened to her.

"Well, that day has come. And I wish it had never come. Now I know Lucia's fate, and it was horrible. It's too much…to find out how she died, how long she's been dead, and not to know it all these years.

"She died five days after she left Lokan for Sinaloa! Ten years she's been dead!"

Tears were filling my eyes and Verónica's too. I knelt beside Carmela, took her hand, and said, "Aunt, God will accompany you through this sorrow. And your brothers and sisters will help you bear the pain. But please tell us what the man told you, how he knew that Lucia died."

Carmela struggled to speak again. When she did, she told us everything that the man had told her. She spared us nothing. As much as I was shocked by the terrible story, I listened with my whole heart because I knew that Verónica would have to write it down and she might need my help. She would have to finish Lucia's story, as sad as the ending would be.

Carmela told us that the Chamula man was called Mateo, and he was with Lucia on the bus to the farm in Sinaloa. They shared a seat for many hours and talked about their families and communities. Mateo had worked several years on the farm, so he told Lucia what to expect, about how they had to sleep on the floor and go to the bathroom in the fields. That must have worried Lucia because it's hard for women to do it modestly.

The bus stopped just once for the workers to go the bathroom by the side of the road. Then a couple hours before daybreak when everyone was asleep, the bus came to an abrupt stop at a roadblock. Two masked men with guns climbed on the bus and demanded that everyone get off.

Mateo and Lucia were just waking up, but they soon realized that something was terribly wrong and quickly joined the other passengers huddled together on the side of the road. They were all whispering about what they thought was happening.

The masked men had partners. They were eight men in all. They shouted to each other in Spanish to divide the people up, nine in each group. Then they pushed the workers like cattle into the back of two vans. Mateo was separated from Lucia in the van, but he could see her. He got her attention so she knew he was there.

Then the driver took off fast down a bumpy road. For about an hour, no one inside the van knew what would happen next. Some of the men said that maybe their captors would demand a ransom to release them. Others said that maybe they would force them to move drugs across the border into the United States. When the van finally stopped, Lucia was praying softly in tsotsil, her head between her knees.

The masked men shouted at everyone to get out of the vans. Mateo and Lucia jumped down and when they landed on the ground their backs met the end of a rifle. They were herded along a path for a couple miles. Light was coming through the trees, and Mateo could see a wooden building ahead. Soon they were inside the building, which was one big room. All eighteen workers, seventeen men, and one woman.

Mateo was very frightened. Nothing had happened to him like this before. He was sitting on the floor beside Lucia afraid to move because the armed men had everyone in a tight circle and were watching every move they made.

Finally the man who seemed to be in charge spoke to the workers. Some of the workers had been right: the armed men belonged to a drug gang, and they had kidnapped the workers to force them to carry drugs across the border.

"You'll make a lot more working for us than you will on the tomato farm," the leader said. Mateo looked around and wondered what the other men were thinking. He knew that he wouldn't work for these men and that Lucia wouldn't either. He didn't know about some of the other men.

The drug gang didn't give the workers any time to decide what they would do. They demanded an answer right away. Either work for the drug gang, or take the consequences. Slowly seven men raised their hands. They agreed to move the drugs across the border. Two masked men led them outside and soon Mateo heard an engine start and a car speed off.

The remaining twelve people kept their hands and heads down. Many crossed themselves and whispered prayers. The masked men didn't do anything with them right away. They left everyone inside the building while they went outside to talk. About fifteen minutes later, one of the men came inside and asked for a volunteer.

When no one volunteered, he grabbed Mateo and pushed him outside. Mateo was terrified when one of the men put a gun to his head. He thought he was going to be shot. But instead another man gave him a can of gasoline and ordered him to pour it all around the house. Then he gave him a match and ordered him to set the house on fire. Mateo couldn't do it and yet he didn't want to die! So he threw the match at the man and ran.

God must have been watching out for him, because Mateo managed to escape the bullets the men shot at him. He ran for a while until he found a hiding place in some bushes. There he watched with terror as the house and everyone inside burned. Mateo held his hands over his ears to stop the screams of the workers, which lasted an eternity, he said. He felt that God had abandoned them.

As soon as the house had burned to the ground, they got into their vans and left. Mateo was afraid they would look for him. But he was lucky. For some reason they didn't.

Finally he got up and ran as fast as he could in the opposite direction of where the men had gone. Although he was in shock and crying as he ran, he didn't stop running until it was dark. He slept in a cornfield that night and many nights after.

He decided to go to El Norte because he was afraid to stay in Sinaloa. A few days later, he reached Altar, Sonora. There he set off across the border with a couple men he had met along the way. They walked in the desert for three days until they came to a place called Tucson. From there Mateo found his way to Atlanta, a big city in Georgia.

For the next ten years he worked in Chinese restaurants all over Georgia. All he did those years was work, as many hours as he could. He sent most of his money to his parents and siblings. Each night when he went to bed, Mateo barely slept. When he managed to fall asleep, he heard the screams of the men and Lucia burning to death and woke up in terror, sweat pouring off his body. He would lie in bed, unable to go back to sleep, until it was time to get up.

Mateo tried lighting candles and praying to God and the father-mother-ancestor-protectors, to free him from his nightmares. But his prayers went unanswered.

Then one morning, he had an idea. He made a promise to God that when he returned to Chiapas, the first thing he would do would be to find all the families of the people who died that day and tell them what happened to their loved ones. The workers were all from Chiapas, and Mateo knew several of the Chamula men. While he was still in Georgia, he called his uncle who got word to the families of these men, and when they heard the news they called Mateo. It was very hard for him to tell them what had happened to their loved ones, but he made himself do it.

The others he started to look for as soon as he got off the bus in San Cristóbal. Carmela was the first person he looked for.

When Carmela finished, I looked at Victorio. We were both shocked that my nightmare had come true. It had predicted how Lucia would die! I knew that Lucia had had the capacity to foresee the future, but I didn't know that I had a similar ability. But it wasn't a gift I wanted.

We took Carmela home with us that afternoon. I didn't want to leave her alone. When we got home, I tried to make her eat. But she only took a few bites of a fried egg and a couple spoons of beans. Before we went to bed, we gathered in front of our altar while Victorio led us in a prayer for Lucia's soul.

Then before I went to the sleeping house, Verónica and I unrolled a couple petates for Carmela and for her and placed them on the ground close to the fire. I thought Carmela needed company that night. Verónica gladly slept beside her, but in the morning she told me that she didn't think she was much company. Each of us felt alone that night. Our bodies may have rested a little, but our souls wandered. Verónica said that she felt as if her soul was running circles around her, searching for something. She didn't know what.

After that sad day, Verónica began to write the last chapter of Lucia's story. She hoped that Diana would let her add it to the book they were making. When she went to the meeting to get feedback on what she had written, she asked Diana if she could add a chapter. Diana said yes, and suggested that Verónica call it an "Epilogue" because it would be in her own words. But Verónica needed to finish it soon, because the book was "going to press." We had never heard that expression before and we liked how it sounded!

As Verónica wrote the last chapter of Lucia's story, she mourned for Lucia. She said that she felt her loss deep in her bones, like she imagines she will feel when I die.

It seemed that I had finished mourning Lucia long ago. Maybe telling her story helped me say goodbye to her. That was good, because I was able to comfort my daughter when a wave of sadness swept over her.

I also comforted Carmela and others in Lokan by organizing a service in the chapel in memory of Lucia. I had never taken charge of a public event before. I took gifts to many people to ask for help with the service. Victorio went with me and everyone said yes.

Almost everyone in Lokan came, even people who don't support the Zapatistas. Lucia had healed anyone who needed her help, and people respected her for that. Madre Evangelina came from Yabteclum and Zapatista representatives from other townships arrived in a couple trucks. Everyone couldn't fit in the chapel, so many sat outside on the grass under a bright blue sky with only a few clouds. Ángel de Jesús prayed a traditional prayer and Victorio read from the Bible. The Catholic women's choir in Lokan sang, the string musicians played sacred music for the Holy Hills, and the guitar group played hymns. It was as it should be, the old and the new blending together, how Lucia had lived her life.

Before the service ended, I thanked everyone for honoring my friend who had given so much to the people of Lokan. My words came straight from my heart, and everyone clapped after I finished.

Later that evening when we were sitting by the fire, Verónica told me something that made me very happy. "Today I felt so proud of you, Mother. You showed everyone that the women of Lokan are true women of the mountains."

EPILOGUE

IN 2008, about a year after I started to tell Lucia's story, the book finally came out. The organization didn't spare any expense to celebrate books! They planned a big party to present the book to the public in a building near the zocalo in San Cristóbal. Verónica and the other writers were told to invite their family and the women they had interviewed. Carmela, Ricardo, Ángel de Jesús, Sebastian, and Victorio and I accompanied Verónica. As we walked through the crowds in the market to the plaza, I overheard Ángel say to Verónica, "See how your family supports you? If only Lucia could hear you read her story. She would be embarrassed, but proud of you at the same time."

Because the celebration happened just before Feast of the Souls, there was an altar and in front of it were candles and pine needles. On top of the altar were marigolds, oranges, bananas, peanuts, tamales, candy, sodas, and many other foods and drinks.

When I saw it, I couldn't believe my eyes, and I exclaimed, "How beautiful they make their altars in the city!" In Lokan, our altars are simple. We only put out a little fruit, candles, tamales, maybe a package of cookies, and some flowers. I wished that we had had a photo of Lucia to put on the altar that night. But all we have are our memories of Lucia's face.

Verónica asked if Diana would let her put a chair in front of the altar for Lucia. Diana liked the idea and brought a chair from her office and put it in front of the altar. It was a wooden one, not a folding chair like the ones we would sit on for the presentation. Diana asked Verónica to tell the people about the chair. "People from other countries will come to our presentation and they may not know what the chair means," she explained.

Verónica sat in the front row with the other authors. I wondered if she felt nervous as the room filled with many kaxlanetik. A group of women in elegant dresses and silk scarves that coiled around their necks talked to each other in a foreign language. Later Verónica found out that these women were from a country called Switzerland, and they had donated money to the organization.

The women whose stories were in the book sat behind the authors in the second row. We parents and other relatives sat in the rows behind them, and everyone else filled the remaining rows. Not many of the women who were interviewed came, even though the organization gave the girls money for the women's transportation to the city.

Some of the girls went to the women's homes to bring them to San Cristóbal, but at the last minute several couldn't go because their children were sick, or someone had died, or who knows what else was happening in their lives. But that was important to remember—books don't matter when you're struggling to keep your children alive. I was glad to hear Diana say that in her introduction.

Verónica was the last person to read. She told me later that it was hard to be last, but she tried to learn from what the other girls did right and wrong in their presentations. When her turn came, she read the part of Lucia's story where I told about how the Virgin Mary had come to her in a dream when she was a little girl. Verónica tried to look up at people from time to time, as Diana had instructed her to do. When she looked at me, I looked straight back at her. I hoped she could see that I had never felt so proud of her. But in truth, I was also worried about how our work had changed Verónica and where it might take her in her life.

After she finished reading, Verónica told everyone why she put the chair in front of the altar and how Lucia had died. I saw tears in many people's eyes! I didn't know that Lucia's story could touch people, make them feel for her.

I pushed my fears down about Verónica's future for the rest of the afternoon while I sampled all kinds of delicious foods from a row of tables on the side of the courtyard. The rest of the family joined me, but they only ate tamales, taquitos, and fruit.

Just before we were ready to leave, Diana came over and introduced herself. She also gave her condolences to us. Then she looked at Verónica and said, "Verónica, I was deeply moved by Lucia's story and your mother's generosity in sharing it. I think you saw that many in the audience were affected by Lucia's life. You have a talent for telling people's stories. I would like you to have the opportunity to develop your gift.

"I want to ask you if you would like to work for the organization full-time. We could use your help in two ways, but you can choose which one is best for you. You could help us put the women's stories into books. You would have to live in San Cristóbal, but you could return to your home on weekends.

"The other option is that you could work in Chenalhó training other girls to record the stories of women in their communities. That way you could live at home. Either way, you'll need to spend a month with us in San Cristóbal learning about the organization and our project. We have a room in the organization's house where you can sleep during the week and on weekends you can return to your family.

"After the training, we'll have meetings in San Cristóbal twice a month with you and two other girls who will train women in Chamula and San Larrainzar. You don't have to tell me your answer right now. But I want to take this opportunity to tell your parents how impressed we are with your work and that we want you to keep working with us."

Verónica looked shocked at Diana's words. I felt my worst fears might come true. We didn't have much time to think because Diana wanted to give us three copies of the book: one for Verónica, one for me, and one for Carmela. We took the books and thanked her. Then Diana said goodbye and moved on to the next girl to meet her family and give them their books.

On the way back to Lokan everyone was chattering about the event, except Verónica and me. I was thinking about what Verónica would decide, how much harder and sadder my life would be if she decided to live in San Cristóbal. I don't know what Verónica was thinking, but her thoughts had taken her far away.

The topic of the job offer didn't come up until Verónica raised it over breakfast the next morning. I was making tortillas when she came into the kitchen and stopped at the altar in the corner. The night before, I had put a copy of our book there. I had hoped that Verónica would see it sharing sacred space with the Bible and a picture of the Virgin of Guadalupe.

Verónica stood at the altar for a while. Then she sat down next to her father who had gotten up early and was drinking his matz. He was about to leave for a meeting in Polhó and didn't have much time to talk.

Verónica cleared her throat before speaking. She spoke more formally than usual.

"Father, Mother, I never thought it would happen, but last night I got a chance to be something more in my life. I want to take this chance, to work full time for Telling Our Stories. But I don't know which job to choose. A part of me wants to live in San Cristóbal to see what life is like there.

"But another part of me feels that I can do something important here with other girls and women. Either way, I'll not be able to help Mother in our store during the week. But I'll have money and can help you and others in our community. What do you think? Should I take the job? Which job should I take?"

We didn't say anything right away. I think we were both collecting our thoughts. Then Victorio said, "Daughter, we don't want you to leave your home again. We remember when you left to live with Rodrigo. You could have died had you stayed with him. We brought you home and after that we never wanted you to leave unless a good man came to ask to marry you.

"But you aren't the same girl who came back to us. You've grown into a strong person who can think for herself and has learned to do many things. Only God knows your destiny. If you feel that he's calling you to live in San Cristóbal, then neither your mother nor I can say that's not true. It seems that the work they want you to do in the organization is like a cargo, even though you'll be paid. You'll serve the original people of Chiapas by recording their stories.

"When others read about us, they'll see that we aren't stupid and uncivilized. Indigenous women are as intelligent as mestizos. Just think about Lucia and your mother! The only difference is that they haven't had the opportunities that mestizas have had. I want you to have opportunities like mestiza girls. I want you to learn. If you want to work in San Cristóbal then you have my blessing. If you want to work here in Chenalhó you know that your mother and I would like that best."

Verónica's whole body seemed to relax. Then she turned to look at me, waiting for what I would say. I think she was most afraid of what her father would say, but also wondering how I would feel about being left alone to care for the house and our store.

But I had changed from the mother Verónica knew when we first started this experiment. Looking back on my life and remembering Lucia had shown me many things, mostly the gains and losses that come with every choice a person makes. I looked into the fire and told my daughter, "You know that once I had a chance to live a different life from other women in Lokan. But my parents wouldn't let me take advantage of that opportunity. I don't want to do the same to you. I don't want anything to keep you from working and learning. I'm not sure where God is leading you or what is in your heart. I don't need to tell you that I would be happy if you stayed in Chenalhó and taught other young women to listen with their whole hearts, as you have listened to me. But whatever you choose, you go with my blessing. I'm proud of you and want you to follow your heart."

Victorio didn't say anything to us when he left, except, "Until later." I think he was worried about losing Verónica forever if she chose to live in San Cristóbal. I got up from where I was sitting by the fire and went to help a customer in the store. I left Verónica sitting by the fire with her thoughts.

About an hour passed before I heard Verónica come down the path to the store and open the door. I was standing on a chair hanging candles on the ceiling with my back to the door. "Hand me those candles, daughter," I told her.

Verónica did as I asked and then said, "Mother, I've been thinking, and I've made my choice."

I got down from the chair and sat down in it, afraid to hear Verónica's decision. She pulled another chair close to me and began to tell me what was in her heart.

"Not long ago I would have done anything to have a job in San Cristóbal and live there all the time. I've dreamt about that, about going to school and working, about selling my weavings to make extra money. I've even thought about how I could have a boyfriend without telling you and Father and having to do joyol!

"When Diana told me about the job, my heart felt like it would burst from all the hopes I've been holding inside me. But now I don't know what's going on with me because I don't feel that much like taking the job in San Cristóbal. Maybe someday I'd like to live there, see how it is, go back to school. But something inside me has changed.

"It seems that now I want to do something here, for my people. Like Father said, if I take the job here it will be like a cargo. Before you told me Lucia's story, I didn't know how important cargos are, that through them we don't just help others, but ourselves. I didn't think one would come to me. Even if it didn't come in a dream, it came in its own way. If I stay in Chenalhó I can help other young women learn the things I've learned."

I was filled with relief and joy to hear Verónica's decision. Before I realized what I was doing, I picked up a candle and put it on the table beside us. Then I asked Verónica to find a match and light it. We knelt there in front of the candle while I prayed to the Moon, Mother Earth, and all the saints and ancestors to bless my daughter in her work.

Verónica's first day of training was in mid-November on a Monday morning. She said goodbye to me early in the morning and assured me that she'd be home on Friday evening. As she was leaving I gave her a little piece of advice: "Listen well, daughter!"

When she returned on Friday she couldn't wait to tell me about her week of training and life in San Cristóbal. I told her to sit down by the fire, pretend I was interviewing her, and give me the long version! She laughed, took a sip of the rice atole I had made for her return, and told me about her week.

"When I got to San Cristóbal I bought a glass of atole and stood for a while drinking it, feeling like one of the many people in the market grabbing some nourishment before going to work. Then I went to the office. Once inside, Diana took me into the library and introduced me to the other team members, Maruch and Herlinda. They would be working in Chamula and San Andrés Larrainzar.

"Maruch gave me a big smile. I was happy that we would be working together. The next day I told her how my cake turned out, and she invited me to go home with her sometime to meet her family.

"The next thing Diana did the first day was tell us about the house. She said that soon after they started the organization, a retired teacher found out about their work and began to donate money to them. She was quite elderly and in time she couldn't live alone in her house. A niece invited the señora to live with her. Instead of selling her house, the señora donated it to the organization.

"Doña Dolores had believed that indigenous girls should have the same rights as mestiza girls, and she had helped many go on in school past sixth grade. Diana pointed to photos on one wall of the study. From inside the row of frames, girls from different townships looked out at me with serious expressions. They held diplomas and all wore their traditional clothes.

"As I gazed up at the photos, I remembered the story of when you and Lucia ran away to San Cristóbal and the señora, Doña Dolores, who gave Lucia work and promised to help her go to school. I asked myself if she could be the same woman who donated this house. I could hardly wait until today to ask you if the last name of Lucia's employer was the same as the woman who owned the house, but I didn't have to wait that long.

"Diana left us to look around in the study at the books and other things Doña Dolores had left behind. I reached for a book lying on its side on top of a row of books and turned the pages of *The Nine Guardians* by Rosario Castellanos. Halfway through the book I came to a piece of folded paper. I opened it up carefully, like an archaeologist discovering an ancient treasure.

"When I had smoothed it out, I saw that it was a letter on lined notebook paper. At the top was "Very esteemed Doña Dolores" and at the bottom was the signature of the letter-writer, Lucia Pérez López. Lucia's signature was made up of little flourishes that rose above and dipped below the line, just as you described it. My heart raced as I read her letter, the one that sealed her fate. I tucked it in the folds of my belt and thought about how you will feel when you see Lucia's signature. Here it is, Mother."

Verónica held out Lucia's letter to me. I didn't take it right away. I couldn't believe that something of Lucia's could still be in the world and had now come back to me.

Finally I took the letter from Verónica and opened it slowly. I didn't want to take the letter in all at once, so I started at the top and worked my way down, reading each line out loud, until I came to Lucia's signature.

It didn't seem possible that lines swirling around each other could bring a person back to life. But Lucia took form before me. She looked at me with her smiling eyes and motioned for me to kneel beside her. I grabbed my shawl from the back of my chair and knelt close to her. I smelled smoke in her hair, smoke from our fire. She reached for my hand.

ACKNOWLEDGMENTS

For their encouragement and close readings of drafts of *When A Woman Rises*, I am deeply grateful to Jena Camp, Elaine Hampton, Bill Jungels, Sandy Marshall, LeeAnn Meadows, Beth O'Leary, Mike O'Malley, Gail Olive Onion, Susan Rivera, Diane Rus, Heather Sinclair, Joanne Townsend, and Carter Wilson. For listening to my earliest musings about this novel, I thank Christine Kovic and participants in a writing workshop in Las Cruces with Denise Chávez. To Lee Byrd, my editor, and to Bobby Byrd and the rest of the team at Cinco Puntos Press, I am forever grateful for the respect you showed me and the culture and people that I portray in this book. Paco Casas and Edgar Amaya took into consideration our ideas and created a book cover that is both beautiful and culturally symbolic.

Lastly, to my friends in San Pedro Chenalhó, Chiapas, Mexico my eternal gratitude for welcoming me into your homes in the 1980s and for teaching me ever since how to laugh and love even in the toughest of times.

CHARACTERS

Lucia: the one who disappeared (born in 1964)
Carmela: Lucia's mother
Pedro: Lucia's father (disappeared in 1969)
Hilario: Lucia's grandfather
Magdalena: Lucia's friend (born in 1964)
Verónica: Magdalena's daughter
Manuel: Magdalena's father
Francisca: Magdalena's mother
Ricardo: Magdalena's older brother
Ernestina: Magdalena's younger sister
Victorio: Magdalena's husband
Abolino and Sebastian: Magdalena's sons
Ángel de Jesús: Lucia's kexol (spiritual and cultural replacement)
Madre Ester: a nun from Mexico City
Doña Dolores: a retired teacher living in San Cristóbal de Las Casas
Diana: director of Telling Our Stories, an oral history project

NOTES

A

agave: A native plant originally from Mexico, member of the Agavaceae family, also known as the century plant or American aloe. Agave has many uses, including using its fibers to make net bags.

antsetike: Plural for women. (tsotsil)

antsil vinik: A gay man. (tsotsil)

atole: A hot drink made with corn or rice. (Spanish)

B

bats'i k'op: "True language," how native speakers of tsotsil refer to their mother tongue. (tsotsil)

Bees, The: A civil society Catholic organization that formed in Chenalhó in 1992 and calls itself *Sociedad Civil Las Abejas* (Civil Society The Bees) for a variety of reasons, one being that like bees they sting the government to make it listen rather than using more aggressive means, such as taking up arms. Bees also make honey, a sweet thing, that Las Abejas members compare to peace and justice, their ultimate goal.

Believers: Followers of *La Palabra de Dios* (The Word of God), the progressive branch of the Catholic Church in Chiapas. In the early 1990s *Pueblo Creyente* (Believing People) began as a broad non-partisan movement of Catholics motivated by the struggle for social justice. In other parts of the world similar expressions of Catholic faith are called Liberation Theology.

bik'it snuk': A falsetto voice of respect used by juniors with seniors and also in certain ceremonies, such as the joyol, or bride petition. (tsotsil)

C

cafetal: Land on which coffee is grown. (Spanish)

Cancún: A city in Yucatán where men from Chiapas migrate in search of work in construction or service jobs.

cargo: A role of service that individuals perform for their communities without remuneration. Cargos may be in governance or in spiritual and health-related matters, such as people who pray for the whole community or for individuals. Members of independent cooperatives and of Zapatista support bases refer to their roles in leadership as cargos. In the past, cargos were usually revealed through dreams, called cargo dreams. (Spanish)

cargo dream: A dream in which a spiritual being comes to a person to give them work to perform for their community. This work was traditionally unremunerated and often still is.

Casa de La Cultura: The House of Culture in the municipal center of San Pedro Chenalhó. (Spanish)

Castellano: A term used by indigenous people to refer to the Spanish language, also called Castillian. (Spanish)

Chamula. An indigenous township of highland Chiapas, Mexico where tsotsil is the original language. Its full name is San Juan Chamula.

Chenalhó: An indigenous township of highland Chiapas, Mexico. It's full name is San Pedro Chenalhó. As part of their colonization plan, the Spaniards created administrative centers in rural areas that they named after Catholic saints who became patron saints of these centers. In tsotsil Chenalhó translates roughly as, "water from a rocky hole in the earth."

chayote: A light green, pear-shaped fruit belonging to the gourd family Cucurbitaceae, along with melons and squash.

chicha: A fermented drink made of sugar cane. (Spanish)

comadre, compadre: A term used to refer to the woman or man who is your son or daughter's godmother or godfather. One can become a godparent at the baptism of a child or at other religious or secular rites-of-passage, such as school graduation. (Spanish)

comal: The clay griddle that tortillas are made on. They come in many sizes, some large enough to prepare tortillas for fiestas. Today most are made of cast iron. (Spanish)

compañeros: Companions in the struggle for a better life. (Spanish)

costal: A large bag made of burlap or other materials to store and carry coffee, corn, sugar, flour, and grains. (Spanish)

D

Doña: An honorific, a term of respect used by mestizos before the first names of women. (Spanish)

E

El Norte: Any place in the United States that migrants go to find work. (Spanish)

elote: Corn fresh from the harvest before it is dried and then cooked with lime to be ground into masa to make tortillas or matz. Elote is either boiled or roasted and is typically eaten by taking off one kernel at a time and putting it in the mouth, rather than bringing the cob to the mouth and biting off the kernels several at a time. (Spanish)

enganchador: A labor contractor, literally a man who "hooks" migrant workers into doing work at a distance from their homes. Enganchadores live either in the regions from where workers migrate or on the farm where workers are headed. (Spanish)

F

Father-Mother-Ancestor-Protectors: Traditional dieties which represent ancestral wisdom and guidance and are often lumped into the tsotsil term kajvaltik.

Feast of the Souls (Sk'in ch'ulelal in tsotsil): Also known as Day of the Dead (*Día de Los Muertos* in Spanish). A tradition in which people welcome back the souls of their deceased loved ones and the ancestors on November 1st and 2nd. The tradition involves visiting cemetaries with gifts of food and flowers and inviting relatives and neighbors to partake of the food on home altars.

flowery face: Words used in prayers to describe the face of God and other Maya and Catholic dieties.

J

j'ak'vomol: A person who uses herbs to heal. Some j'ak'vomol also use massage and steam baths. (tsotsil)

j'ilol: A traditional healer who heals with prayer; one who "sees." Plural, j'iloletike. (tsotsil)

joyol: The traditional process through which young men petition to marry (tsotsil)

K

kaxlan: A descendent of colonists and people of European descent. The plural form is kaxlanetike. (tsotsil, "x" is pronounced like "sh")

kexol: A person who bears a similarity to another person or is considered to be able to replace them. (tsotsil, "x" is pronounced like "sh")

L

Lokan: The fictional name of one of the 100 or so small communities in the township of San Pedro Chenalhó. (tsotsil, means "Let's go!")

lum: The municipal center of a township, with stores, churches, schools, a clinic, and government offices. In the case of Chenalhó, the lum refers to the municipal center of the original administrative center in the township of San Pedro Chenalhó. In 1995 another administrative center was established in Polhó, the center of the Autonomous Zapatista township of San Pedro Polhó, which is located within the boundaries of San Pedro Chenalhó. There are 38 autonomous Zapatista townships across the state of Chiapas. (tsotsil)

M

madres: The Spanish term used by native people in Chenalhó to refer to Catholic nuns.

masa: Corn dough used to make tortillas, tamales, and matz (Spanish)

matz (mats): Coarsely ground corn mixed with water and drunk throughout the day, a staple of the diet in Maya communities. (tsotsil). Maya writers of tsotsil now replace "ts" instead of "tz" in an effort to decolonize their language. In *When a Woman Rises*, the old spelling for matz is used to help distinguish it from the English word, mats.

mayol: A young man who keeps the peace and cleans up after fiestas. This cargo fills some of the functions of a policeman, but is not a full-time or paid position. A mayol doesn't carry a gun, but instead a hard wood baton or night stick. (tsotsil)

me' max: The wife of a man whose nickname is max, meaning "monkey", a type of dancer who has a cargo in some religious festivals. Me' is a female marker in tsotsil.

mestizo (mestiza, feminine): A non-indigenous person. (Spanish)

mol: An honorific, used before the first name of respected older men. (tsotsil)

moy: Wild tobacco, considered to be a powerful diety. (tsotsil)

N

nagual: An animal spirit companion, born at the same time as a person is born and which shares the person's fate. The nagual has the power to leave the body and walk around, especially during states of sleep and drunkenness. (Nahuatl, a language of central Mexico)

níspero, loquat (Eriobotrya japonica): A tree that produces a small, round, or pear-shaped fruit. In Lokan, the fruit is white or yellow and the skin is yellow.

P

petate: A straw mat used for various purposes, including sleeping and sorting beans. (Spanish)

pinole: Parched corn, dried, ground, and mixed with water and sugar to make a drink.

pitch pine: A tree whose bark can be used as a torch or to light fires.

Polhó: The political and ceremonial center of the Autonomous Zapatista township of San Pedro Polhó. Founded in 1995.

pox: Alcohol distilled from sugar cane juice used as an offering in petitions for spiritual help and social support. Also the tsotsil word for medicine. (tsotsil)

Pueblo Creyente: See *Believers*.

R

resistance, the: A movement inspired by the formation of autonomous Zapatista townships in which those involved do not take any form of government assistance (e.g. cash, food, tin for roofs, cement for floors) based on the belief that the Mexican government has used this aid to buy the submission of the poor and the original people of Chiapas and Mexico.

rotoplas: A polyethelene container to collect rain water. (Spanish)

S

San Cristóbal de Las Casas: The urban center of the highlands of Chiapas where Spanish colonists based themselves after invading the region. It was originally called Cuidad Real and was founded in 1528. Today San Cristóbal is home to many migrants from rural areas who have established settlements on its periphery. The city is also a popular tourist destination.

Sinaloa: A Mexican state in the North of Mexico.

Subcommander Marcos: Subcommander of the Zapatista Army of National Liberation from the inception of the movement until 2014. Marcos is the nom-de-guerre of a mestizo philosophy professor from central Mexico who answered the call of Bishop Ruíz, the Bishop of

Chiapas from 1959-1999, to come to Chiapas in the early 1980s and do community organizing among the most marginalized people.

support bases: Groups of men, women, and young adult supporters of the Zapatistas who work together to realize the social, political, and economic goals of the Zapatista movement.

T

tamales: Corn dough filled with beans, either ground or whole, wrapped in a leaf and steamed. Tamales eaten in Lokan rarely have meat in them, but sometimes they have greens.

traditional ones, traditionalists: Original people of Chenalhó who maintain an intimate relationship with Maya dieties and Catholic saints which they have worshipped side-by-side since the Spanish invasion.

tsotsil: One of several Mayan languages spoken in Chiapas. (native speakers refer to their language as bats'i k'op or "true language")

V

vinikitike: Plural for men. (tsotsil)

W

Word of God (*La Palabra de Dios* in Spanish): The Catholic social justice movement in Chiapas which began in the 1960s under the guidance of Bishop Samuel Ruíz García. The word of God also refers to passages in the Bible.

Z

Zapatistas: Civilian supporters of the EZLN, the Zapatista Army of National Liberation, which rose up on January 1, 1994 against neoliberal capitalism and the Mexican state's failure to respect the rights of the original peoples of Mexico.

zocalo: The central park of a Mexican city, town, or village, traditionally a gathering place on Sunday evenings. (Spanish)

Photo by Mike O'Malley

In 1987, CHRISTINE EBER lived for a year with a family in San Pedro Chenalhó, doing fieldwork for her PhD in Anthropology. She shared daily life with women and their families, witnessing the difficulties they faced. It changed her life. Now, as a respected anthropologist, she continues to work with the indigenous women of Chiapas, visiting communities on a regular basis and supporting the woman-organized weaving collectives. Her most recent book is *The Journey of a Tzotzil-Maya Woman: Pass Well Over the Earth*, which she co-authored with Antonia. She lives in Las Cruces, New Mexico, with her husband, Mike, and dog Sami.